Izzy Come . . .
Izzy Go

By
Jennifer Rae

Copyright Notices

©Jennifer Rae Trojan

Published under the Copyright Laws of the Library Of Congress of The United States of America by:

Jennifer Rae Trojan Publishing
West Chicago, Illinois
kessenskronikles@gmail.com

International Standard Book Number
(ISBN) 978-0-692-53278-2

Also by Jennifer Rae:
Kessen's Kronikles,
The Adventures of a Cross Country Canine

Disclaimer

This is a work of fiction. Names, characters, places, events and incidents are either the products of the author's imagination or used in a fictitious manner.

Cover Photo

©2014 by Stephanie D. Ascencio–Schmoopsie Pet Photography

Cover Design

©2015 by Pam Osbourne

DEDICATION

To My Husband Chuck

Who:

Encourages my every endeavor…

Adds laughter and humor to my day…

Is my best friend in the whole world…

And to top it all…

Loves me to bits.

FIRST IMPRESSIONS

She touched down that late afternoon like a dark funnel cloud...whirling around the kitchen, crashing into things and creating a path of destruction. My life will never be the same.

Kessen

A black blur with paws was now twirling around the room at speeds greater than sound. Kessen sees her as trouble in the making. I see her as a mini-me and potential mischief-maker of my liking.

Brightie

OMG! What have we gotten ourselves into this time?

Mom and Dad

TABLE OF CONTENTS

INTRODUCTION

Although the air is relatively calm, the slight whistling of the tree branches sets the scene for this special time on the deck in my dog run…it's storytelling time. Twinkling stars surrounding the full, golden moon create the perfect setting for this special event. The dogs of the neighborhood gather here and, in doing so, forfeit their last exercise of the night in hopes of hearing an exciting story. Waiting patiently for the arrival of the host and storyteller, their anticipation of an exciting tale keeps them coming back for more each week. However, my canine audience is in for quite a surprise with this particular evening's adventure…something they have never experienced nor anticipated during storytelling time.

Those anxious pooches crowding the deck are waiting for me. I am the resident host and eager storyteller in the neighborhood, and it is a responsibility that I take most seriously. While having a flair for words, vocal excitement and a vivid imagination are all part of being a success, my canine credentials are important as well. Having said that, please allow me to introduce myself. My name is Kessen, and I am a mix between a Golden Retriever and a Labrador Retriever. I was a potential assistance dog but had a change of career to become a therapy dog. My life's adventures were also featured in a book with me as the storyteller. In addition to those qualifications, as the senior, male, canine member of what I refer to as the sorority house, I see puppies come and go through turnstile-type chapters in my life as well as in theirs. My stories come alive through their adventures, and tonight, I am the host of yet another puppy escapade...one that not only shatters the serenity of the household but changes it in many ways.

I owe my vast puppy experiences to my mom and dad. As puppy raisers for an organization that breeds, raises, trains and donates dogs to the disabled, they bring a puppy into our lives for a period of about fifteen months. My best friend and adopted sister named Brightie and I help the folks prepare the pup for Advanced Training or Puppy College as it's called. As

volunteers, our parents register the puppy in obedience classes, teach a variety of basic but important commands, are totally responsible for public etiquette and strive for proper leash behavior. These people have fifteen months to accomplish their goals, and they do it with a bit of canine assistance. That's where Brightie and I lend our paws and expertise to the endeavor.

Would my mom and dad be able to do this as well without canine intervention? I think not, and that's why assistance is provided by our team known as the Socialization Squad. Brightie and I formed this squad a few years ago and work together as co-captains to help with the pups. As a team, we teach the pups in training what only dogs can teach each other well. We focus on bite inhibition, appropriate dog to dog interaction and pack behavior. I truly believe that humans can't do this as well as we can. To some extent they are successful, but truth be told, these skills belong entirely to the canines of the world.

Please forgive me if I seem pompous. I'm told by Brightie that I often project a haughty demeanor, but I seriously don't mean to appear that way, nor do I feel I am as pretentious as she perceives. I'm the only male canine in a household full of females. Believe me…it's a struggle not only to mediate the raucous interactions that occur on a daily basis but also to maintain my position in the pack as the senior, canine member of the household. Fortunately, I'm older and have a bit more self-control then the "ladies of the doghouse." My alleged, arrogant demeanor is my only defense against the femme fatales of the canine persuasion in residence. While my beliefs might offend the female dogs of the world, they come from extensive experience in this sorority house that I call my home, and my survival as pack leader depends upon it.

In spite of the occasional chaotic atmosphere, I love my home, my responsibilities as part of the household as well as my role as storyteller. I go way back in terms of visiting dogs, and my memory is just as sharp as it was years ago when I assumed ownership of the storytelling role. It comes easily for me since I play an integral part of the experiences. I have a talent for keeping dogs of all ages on the edge of their hind quarters while listening to my imagination go wild with tales of the unexpected. On storytelling night, my listeners sit at the edge of the deck in the dog run with eyes glistening, tails wagging with anticipation and hearts fluttering with excitement. Their paws tingle and hackles quiver with thoughts of tales to come, and my imagination never lets them down. (*Now that really sounds pompous.*)

This evening's story is meant for one such balmy night when the usual barking dogs in the neighborhood are fast asleep, and only the eager listeners congregate at the edge of the deck in the dog run. The once, magnificent moon now casts an ominous shadow through the tree's branches as my audience anxiously awaits the unfolding of the story. It's of a most unusual pup who alters the serenity of our safe haven through mischief and mayhem. This is, indeed, a story worthy of their anticipation. As I stare into their eager eyes making each visitor feel as though I am staring into their souls and singling them out for such an exciting adventure, I begin the tale of escapades well beyond their beliefs. It's one that might even be the best story ever told.

Tonight, however, my involvement has a different twist in that it only serves as an introduction to the main character's unique arrival years ago. Relinquishing my role as storyteller is the surprise mentioned earlier and allows me to leave the sharing of the actual adventure to her...our weekend guest and former member of the sorority house. I admit that this tactic is both a tease and a cheap trick on my part. My hope is that by telling a little bit about her chaotic arrival as a pup, it sets the stage for her personal telling of the story in a very different order, gives insights into her motivation as well as demonstrates her intense belief in possibilities.

A hush falls over my audience as I assume my regal, storyteller stance on the deck. (*There I go sounding a bit pretentious again, but I just can't help myself.*) The slight, unexpected breeze causes a bit of tingling in the hackles of the listeners, and that is the surprising yet perfect cue for me to begin my part of the adventure.

The day is Valentine's Day…a day when red collars and leashes are brought out for that special parade through the neighborhood. Red bandanas are wrapped strategically around the necks of the numerous canines on their strolls. While the pups enjoy way too many special treats, their proud parents etch the memory of the day into history with their cameras.

It's a truly glorious day until dusk, and that's when suddenly everything changes. As evening approaches, our parents bring a new puppy to the sorority house. In hindsight, Brightie and I should have anticipated this new arrival since gates appeared tactically placed around the house, small crates were visible in various corners of rooms, and low-standing food bowls had been positioned next to our elevated ones. The comfort of our daily routines clouded our situational awareness, and that misguided ease even fooled our hackles. That instinctual warning system usually alerts us to various situations and rarely misleads us. This time, however, we were all fooled from neck to tail.

This female newcomer is a tiny pup, and her coal-black coat camouflages her dark piercing eyes that seem to dart all over the place while taking everything in at a mere glance. With her triangular-shaped head held high, suggesting a slight arrogance on her part, she surveys the house and looks each of us over as though she has already vetted us by some sort of canine system of investigation. Having done this, she takes off in whirlwind-like fashion in her attempt to survey her new digs...dismissing us without even a proper greeting. Like a harsh tornado swooping through the house, she leaves destruction in the form of disheveled throw rugs and couch pillows. An ill-planned hurdle over an elevated food bowl stand sends the bowls crashing to the floor. The falling bowls from their lofty height shatter the stillness of the night with their noisy, staccato-like clanking across the ceramic floor tiles, while the stand lands upside down on the floor. How can such a little pup cause this level of chaos in such a short period of time?

The earlier stillness that filled the air surrounding the deck is now broken as the listeners' imaginations run wild with anticipation of what is to come. Paws tingling and

We're safe up here on the couch!

hackles on full alert reveal their excitement as the adventure unfolds. (*Let's face it...a pup running wild through a house is always exciting.*)

Now, I have different thoughts about this mysterious, new pup. I think that she is mega-trouble in canine form and admit to feeling a vague sense of unrest that somehow frightens me. The bristling hackles on my neck are proof of that, and my hackles are almost never wrong…well, almost never. Brightie, whose name might have been Mischief-Maker, believes that she sees her soul mate in this explosive, black gust of wind and is anxious to learn more about her. Our mom and dad are stunned by the pup's most unusual antics. Their eyes glaze over as they realize that this new member of the sorority house, who is currently thrashing around the perimeter of rooms and bouncing off walls and doors, will be in residence for the next fifteen months. Even the sky, once filled with sunshine on this almost perfect Valentine's Day, is now shrouded by darkened clouds. Might that ominous change be a clear warning of what is to come?

As the dogs on the deck listen attentively so as not to miss what happens next, I have to remind myself as well as my audience not to allow first impressions to cloud their perception of this new arrival. Even I must remain objective, as one who not only provides the background information, but one who is also an active participant in this particular adventure. The listeners on the deck need to learn more about this mysterious, black gust of wind who is flying back and forth at speeds rarely attempted in the house. To accomplish this and in fairness to the main character, we'll hear her version of the adventure as she chooses to tell it. I'm sure you will agree that this is a most unusual way to tell a story, but in this case, it will all come together in the end. Will the events of her story alter perceptions of her? Only time will tell…

While the visiting dogs find comfortable spots on the deck, they extend their paws for comfort and wiggle close to each other not knowing what storytelling twists and turns await them. I continue my introduction, unlike any story that I have ever shared, and one that might remain in their minds as well as yours, the reader, for quite some time. It's all about this new, mysterious puppy and how she changes our lives forever.

As I prepare to relinquish my role as storyteller to the main character, my audience gets their first glimpse of this black tornado who jostled the serenity of our household. A sudden hush settles over the listeners as she enters the deck area, and their hackles are going wild due to the excitement of seeing her for the first time. Her coal-black coat against the darkness of the night creates the illusion of a shadow-like creature stepping confidently into the spotlight. As she is about to assume the role of storyteller, she positions herself next to me, and out of respect for my position in the household, awaits my signal to begin.

Before making any judgments about her, I ask that you first listen to her version of the story. Please keep in mind that first impressions aren't always a true indicator of one's character. That being said, I'll let our storyteller begin her adventure as only she can tell it…

PART I
THE EVENT
(Fifteen Months Later)

The anticipation is almost too much for me as I await the final challengers' results in this ultimate competition. My paws are actually sweating, my hackles are overworked, and I do believe that I might drool if I open my mouth. I'll never make the cover of Dog World magazine looking like that!

Since I was a young puppy, I have been working and training for this particular day...the day of the event that might change my life forever, and there's no going back from this day's outcome. I can hardly contain my exhilaration as I try to shake off the nerves that seem to be taking control of my senses. This day is the culmination of everything I have dreamt about and worked towards...against all odds. By all odds, I mean that this moment in time is not my pre-determined destiny. In fact, it is probably the farthest career choice in everyone's mind except mine.

During the past fifteen months, I've been living with a wonderful foster family who has other plans for my life. As puppy raisers for an assistance dog organization, they are preparing me to be an assistance dog for a disabled person. That is supposed to be my destiny, but it isn't a direction I might choose for myself. While a career in service is probably the most admirable option that any dog might select, I just didn't feel that it was right for me. I have very different goals.

Jennifer Rae

My career choice, shallow as it may seem, pales in comparison to service and is probably looked upon as highly superficial in terms of significance. From the time I was eight weeks old, I was able to jump effortlessly into the air and out run any pup in the kennel. These talents brought me total happiness, and I believe that I may use my abilities as a means of becoming a winner...a champion in some event that utilizes these skills that bring me such great joy.

Looking back, I wasn't an easy pup by any stretch of the imagination. I challenged my foster parents in every way possible just so they might share in my dreams. My lack of cooperation took the form of refusals; and, might I add, I was quite the achiever in that area. For example, I'd run into my kennel when I saw my leash, refuse to get out of the car, crouch in the middle of the street, hug the pavement during walks and execute many other refusal techniques. My tool box was a treasure chest full of refusal skills, but my family came here today, in spite of my defiance, to support my hard work and efforts toward my chosen goals.

Mom is acting as my handler since I can't do this alone. Believe me, convincing her to be a part of my dream was not an easy task. My not being able to communicate verbally with people, let alone speak Human, was the biggest of my hurdles in terms of convincing her. Let's face it...this was not going to be easy. My mom was one tough coach, and her tool box of training methods was, and still is, much bigger than mine. I had to find a way to communicate my dreams to her. With the help of my foster siblings, Kessen and Brightie, I somehow managed to accomplish this. We're here today at this championship competition as a family, and it looks like my dreams are coming true. Competitive agility is without a doubt my ticket to stardom.

I have to force myself to pay attention, shake off these nerves and not let my anxiety take me back to memories of my past. That trip down memory lane is just too distracting. My competition scores still have me in first place, but two other dogs have yet to compete. They are the two greatest competitors from my agility class. The first is a beautifully marked, black and white Border Collie named Jax. He is known for his incredible speed and stealth-like closeness to the ground when he runs. The other is a white and rust-colored Jack Russell Terrier named Flip who jumps like she has wings! A simple mistake on their parts like missing a turn due to excessive speed or losing focus because of something happening in the arena might just be my golden ticket to the championship title. We have competed together before in previous classes and know each other's weaknesses. I'm just hoping that I can keep my first place position.

The attention is now on the arena as Jax takes to the course. He is definitely off to a great start, but just as he is about to make a critical turn, Jax catches sight of the most gorgeous Miniature Poodle that he has ever seen. She's sitting on the sidelines, and her immaculately coifed poodle-cut only intensifies the contrast between her snow-white coat and her penetrating "come to me" canine eyes. For just a split-second, Jax is smitten and loses his focus on the course. Even though he quickly regroups, critical seconds are lost, and his only hope is that he might make up the time with speed and intensity. Jax finally completes the course and assumes a perfect sitting position on the pause table. It's evident by his demeanor that he isn't as confident with his performance today as he has been in other competitions. That petite temptress of a poodle was quite the ultimate distraction for him, and Jax is not accustomed to losing his focus.

Flip is the final competitor. With absolute certainty, I know that she isn't going to allow that diminutive, catalog queen in a poodle-cut to distract her. She saw what happened to Jax and is strictly business as she speeds through the course...never losing eye contact with her handler. However, that intensity causes another lapse in focus of a different nature. Catching a slight glimpse of multi-colored balloons fluttering in the crowd makes her misjudge one of her hurdles, and she accidently taps the bar with her hind legs as she sails over the top. That lapse in focus costs her some critical points in a very close competition. She never made that mistake before in high level trials, but she still has the speed and high scores for the total course to perhaps see her through to the first place position. Now, it's all in the hands of the judges, and the suspense is pawsitively nerve-racking!

As the judges tally the scores, I find myself gasping for air in an attempt to maintain my composure. Calming myself with deep breaths that either mimic reverse sneezing or an asthma attack seems to help. My breathing gradually returns to a somewhat normal state, and I feel the calming self-control returning to my senses. What is happening to me? I need to get a firm paw-hold on my emotions, or everything I have worked for will be in vain.

In an attempt to regain my composure, I look out at the crowded arena, and my thoughts wander to some of the adventures I've had during my journey to this competition. Not only do I see my dad, other relatives, Kessen and Brightie in one section of the arena, but also some dogs that I have met in my travels. How nice of them to come and see me in this most challenging event of my life.

He's so cute!

Riggins, a handsome Golden Retriever with a great sense of humor, is sitting with Cousin Carolyn, Cousin Steven, Auntie Carol and Auntie Fran in the fourth row of the arena. When my folks sponsored an agility play date in the yard a few months ago, Cousin Carolyn introduced me to Riggins. He and I shared an immediate connection, became great friends and gave the words "play date" new meaning. What was initially meant as play time for us turned into what we later thought of as our very first date...perhaps even a promise of a future relationship when we are older. Seeing him today with his family gives me such hope for the future...our future together after I win this championship competition. I'll become a famous agility competitor and maybe even have my own tour bus! Wait a minute! The stress of this competition is making me lose my paw-hold on reality! I'm still attempting to catch my breath let alone thinking of my own tour bus!

Suddenly, I see Deon...the regal yellow Labrador Retriever who is actually the first service dog that I have ever met. We encountered each other at a fund raiser for an assistance dog organization about five months ago. As I recall, we chatted for quite some time about his important responsibilities as a service dog and silent guardian to his partner. His pride in this career choice was most evident, and in some ways, I envied his convictions. In hindsight, his thoughts made me think about my options. From time to time after that meeting, I do admit to having misgivings about my current career choice.

He's such a wise canine.

Some of Deon's beliefs were often shared by others. Kessen, my adopted brother, always reminded me to keep my options open, and he believed that I needed to be careful about my choice of careers. According to him, I had been making wrong decisions since the first day I joined the family. (*Was he kidding?*) Aren't a championship trophy and blue ribbon worth the effort when a dream comes true? Somehow saying it out loud makes it seem less important and ever so shallow. Sounding so superficial really makes me question my goals. It's possible that I really don't know who I am or what is best for me and for my future. This day is turning into a thought provoking experience rather than a celebration of hard work and effort.

On the other paw, my adopted sister Brightie keeps telling me to go for it. Brightie, being the resident diva in the household, and I share the same views about winning, success, trophies and ribbons. The more ribbons on the kennel walls, the bigger the boost to one's self esteem...not to mention the calming effect on one's inner self. According to Brightie, multiple blue ribbons adorning kennel walls are the height of perfection in canine feng shui and lend harmony to the environment. In her philosophy of life, there's no better wallpaper than ribbons...especially the blue ones. She and her views are so inspirational, and there is no question that she and I are truly soul mates! On the other paw, I must also consider the fact that Brightie is the only canine who shares that point of view with me, and there's not too much credibility in those numbers.

She's such a stunning canine.

As I attempt to settle my nerves, I once again look into the crowd and see another familiar face. She's a really gorgeous, caramel-colored Golden Retriever named Kelyna who happens to be an assistance dog for the hearing impaired. While she takes in the sights and sounds of the arena, her flowing golden coat glistens with each graceful turn of her head. There is an impish quality about her that is reflected in her sparkling, penetrating eyes. As she looks intently at me, I feel like she's looking right through me. Her energy just makes my hackles quiver, and I do believe that she puts the wow in bow-wow. While I am sure that she is hoping for my success today, I have a hunch that she also hopes that I am making the right decision in terms of careers. We met a few months ago at a dog walk, and the pride she had in her service career made my efforts towards competition success look much too shabby in comparison.

She's so beautiful.

A few rows down from Kelyna is a statuesque English Golden Retriever named Carlita. She is also a service dog who was partnered with a returning veteran. I'm surprised that she can take her eyes off him long enough to look at me while waiting for my results. Her partner is quite handsome, and Carlita is pretty easy on the eyes as well. In fact, one might say that she is "drop the bone" gorgeous. Her appearance is breathtaking. While I need as much of my breath as I can manage under this competition stress, I can't help but risk yet another breathing episode by staring at her. The velvet texture of her ears only accentuates the almond color of her coat, and her eyes have this penetrating quality that make my paws sweat just looking at her. (*My paws tend to sweat a lot when under stress!*) I do so want to look like her, but reality hits me smack dab in the muzzle. She's delicate, and I'm athletic. How can I best describe it? She's couture, and I'm retail!

Wanting to look like Carlita reminds me of the first time we met. It was a seminar for potential assistance dogs that was conducted by a visiting, certified dog trainer named Jan from North Carolina. Jan happened to be friends with my folks and coincidently had also been the puppy raiser and trainer for Kelyna.

During the seminar, there were various demonstrations by trainers, but the one conducted by Jan with Carlita was the most memorable. As Jan took Carlita through various commands, it was evident that Carlita was remarkable not only in her quick response and eye contact but also in her obvious enjoyment of being a working dog. Here was a puppy who really enjoyed what she was doing. Seeing her today, fully trained and in this new role as a service dog, was way beyond impressive in my thoughts about her. It almost makes me want to be just like her, but that would mean giving up my dreams of athletic glory, and I'm not sure I'm ready to do that at this point in my life.

Are all these service dogs naturally so beautiful? Is wearing a signature cape making a dog in uniform more striking or is the job they do for others making them more attractive and likely to make my lips quiver? What's with all of these service dogs showing up to wish me well? Is fate sending me a message in the form of a canine intervention?

Seeing my family, friends and these magnificent service dogs makes me want to go back in time and really think about what I am doing with my life. This competition is what I believed to be the most important day of my life…the one I have worked for during the last fifteen months. Why then do I have this intense desire to go back to my beginnings…to my puppy days when my life was easy and uncomplicated? I was an energetic, jumping pup believing in dreams. Why am I so confused and questioning my goals? This is my big day, and I'm supposed to be happy.

Now, the judges have completed their calculations and are moving toward the three of us. Due to the anticipation of the results, Jax, Flip and I are on the edge of our paws. One judge holds this magnificent trophy and the others grip the cherished ribbons signifying first, second and third place. As they approach, I find my mind once again drifting back to the very beginning of my journey. I attempt to focus on that shiny blue ribbon in the hands of the judge. Somehow, everything is becoming hazy. My mind is playing ridiculous tricks on me since I no longer see the judges but glimpses of my youth. Have these past fifteen months of effort and training taken me in the wrong direction? If that were true, do I still have a chance to make it right?

Through the haze of this nervousness and uncertainty that has overcome me, I once again see myself as that

Will looking back to my younger days help?

incorrigible, young puppy in the kennel that I considered my first home. Will reliving those months in my mind help me trust the choices I have made, or might that exploration change my direction entirely?

The judges are getting closer, and I can almost feel the luxurious, blue, satin ribbon going around my neck. If I win this, there is no turning back. I'll have no chance for a career in assistance. Panic is overtaking me as I question everything that I believed to be right for me. Is winning what I really want, or through some twist of fate, have I come to appreciate and choose a different way of life? Do I even have time to change my mind? I seem to lose myself in thoughts of my early days as a young puppy. In the midst of my mind's confusion, I can't even remember my name...

PART II
THE JOURNEY BEGINS
(Fifteen Months Earlier)

My name is Izzy.

1

Follow the Dreams

My name is Izzy...it's not short for Isabelle or Isabella. It's just Izzy. My foster parents, who are puppy raisers for an assistance dog organization, gave me this name when they picked me up from the kennel. You see, I am a foster pup who is being raised as a potential assistance dog...one whose life is entrusted to strangers who promise to take care of me for the next fifteen months of my life and prepare me for a goal of the organization's choosing. I suppose that sounds much too cynical, but it's just a reflection of my skeptical nature. At this point in my young life, I'd really prefer to have some say in my own future.

Telling you a little about me and how it all began might be helpful in terms of understanding my situation and point of view. I'm not the precious-looking, eight week old puppy whose antics and puppy breath seem to draw oohs and aahs from humans. I'm fourteen weeks old and one of the more mature pups who spent those precious ooh and aah weeks in a kennel setting. However, I believe that I am quite attractive with my glossy black coat, piercing eyes, pearly white teeth and a somewhat angular face. I exude mystery in both my appearance and demeanor, and while sounding pretentious, the truth is my only defense.

I might add to the drama by saying that I spend my days just waiting for someone to choose me above the tiny pups who reside in the kennels a few weeks after their births. You know the ones...the cute, pudgy ones who are readily snatched up by parents longing for a forever pup. But, I won't go that melodramatic route just yet because I'm saving that for a time when it is most effective.

Truth be told, I fully enjoy my kennel time. What's not to enjoy? I have daily food, access to play with my two, remaining littermates, no specific rules to follow and secret, life-changing goals that I only share with my best friend who just happens to be my brother. I am a free spirit who frolics within the kennel's confines and play yard. What's more, I don't know any other way of life. As far as I am concerned, my life is carefree, wonderful and full of potential. Of course, the weather leaves a lot to be desired, but the snow and chilling winds that smack the Midwest can't possibly last forever.

My siblings and I said good bye to our mother weeks ago just before we came to this kennel. Sadness as well as fear overcame us as we said our last goodbyes. What would we do without her motherly protection and guidance? She taught us so many wonderful things during our time with her. She encouraged us not to be frightened of those pointed things growing inside our mouths called teeth which were very necessary for our own personal growth. They must have been very painful for her in terms of her feeding us as we grew a bit older. On the other paw, they helped with our transition to regular puppy food; so I guess the end justified the means.

I'm sure our mother had a different perspective on it, but she put our needs above her own comfort. That's just what mothers do for their litters.

She also taught us to venture out beyond our safe enclosure, to let the pads of our paws feel the coolness of the fallen snow or even enjoy catching snowflakes in our mouths as they gently fell from the sky. Her goal was for us to savor the adventures that life has to offer as independent pups. While sharing at the communal food bowl wasn't a lesson well-learned by us, being on time when our food tumbled into the huge bowl was a priority. Food was definitely at the very top of our priority list. While we had the attention span of gnats, we did learn to get to the food bowl on time. Nevertheless, I do believe that our mom's greatest gift to us was the confidence she instilled through her love and guidance. While a few of my littermates remained shy and tentative, my remaining siblings and I felt totally prepared for the adventures that the world had to offer.

I love my brother and sister.

One by one, my tiny littermates were selected by families looking for cute and cuddly puppies. However, my brother, sister and I stayed in the kennel. Both of my remaining siblings have coats that are black as coal just like mine, and sometimes I imagine that their bright white teeth might glow in the dark. But I don't dare to sneak a peek at them during the night for fear that might be true. Actually seeing teeth that glow in the dark would be much too creepy...even for me, and I thrive on foolish notions.

I am so lucky to have such beautiful siblings. Since they don't have people-given names yet, I gave them the

Activity is not her specialty.

kennel names of Calm and Calmer based upon their behavior. Calm, who is a bit smaller than Calmer, just wants to eat and sleep. If she could do both at the same time, I do believe that she would. Her life's goals are somewhat limited...to say the least.

Calmer, on the other paw, is a low-keyed sort of pup, but he also has goals. His primary goal at this point in time is to find the best spot to sleep indoors or outside in the sunshine. He doesn't do that just so he can sleep peacefully but, in fact, uses the solitude and comfort of a quiet spot for his thoughts. You see, Calmer is a bit of a thinker. While very soft-spoken, he often talks about his special dream of someday helping others. I like to share secrets with him since Calm is always asleep somewhere and probably couldn't keep

He is definitely a thinker.

a secret anyway. She is never awake long enough to hear gossip let alone share it with others. I guess one might say that Calmer is my very best friend and confidant.

I am, of course, the opposite in terms of behavior. Nothing is more exciting to me than outdoor escapades. Sleep is overrated as far as I am concerned especially since the snow-filled yard has so many opportunities for exploration. Once I am outside, my imagination soars, and off I go to some corner of the yard either chasing an invisible intruder or some ominous creature hiding in the low, snow-covered bushes. Running close to the ground like a stealth bomber through the mounds of snow is my specialty, and I often corner my target using serpentine maneuvers. Of course, the target tends to be

My imagination runs wild in the snow.

just a lingering leaf or a branch that has fallen from one of the snow-laden trees, but that never disappoints me. The pursuit is what gets my hackles up from neck to tail, and the exhilaration of the capture is what I consider the marrow in the dog bone. I thought this carefree life of mine with my brother and sister would last forever. We had it all or so I thought. Then, everything changed.

Foster parents were looking for a female, black Labrador Retriever to raise as a potential assistance dog. Although I was older than they expected, I fit the bill in terms of gender, color and breed. What more did they want? Didn't they know that compromise is a part of life? (*There I go sounding cynical again, but sometimes, I just can't help myself.*)

On the other paw, I am touted as petite, smart, sweet, but a bit of a jumper. Yes...I am petite, definitely smart and somewhat sweet, but I take exception to being referred to as a bit of a jumper. That is quite an understatement since I take jumping very seriously and am proud of it. I have world championship potential in terms of jumping, and that is a fact.

My goals include numerous possibilities, and all are fashioned around my incredible jumping capabilities and speed. I have the potential to become a talented disc dog. For those who don't know of this activity, disc dog competition, not to be confused with disco, is a competitive sport involving dogs catching flying discs while in midair at great heights and distances. Winning the title of Midwest Champion Disc Dog is comparable to winning the gold medal in the human Olympics. I have what it takes to go the distance in terms of high jumping, twirling and twisting. I can peel the paws off a Jack Russell Terrier in terms of parallel jumping and still have a lot of growing to do.

I am also considering dock diving since my long jumps are the best and longest in the play yard. While I've never jumped into water, I believe it is similar to jumping into a much larger version of a bath tub while chasing a toy. That doesn't sound very difficult to me. I've only had a few baths in my short life, and although I'm not that crazy about water, I can overcome that issue if championship glory is in my sights. If nothing else, I am a believer in myself.

My final interest is in competitive agility. This activity incorporates all of my athletic skills...jumping over hurdles, maneuvering through tunnels, balancing on an elevated beam, scaling a seesaw as well as conquering other obstacles. Speed is the key to success in that area, and I definitely have speed. So far, competitive agility is my favorite, but I want to keep my options open while I'm young. Age and maturity will only help my athletic capabilities in whatever area I select.

That's my future as I see it, and I have plans to make it happen. I fully intend to work towards my goals by running laps, stretching and jumping as much as I can. After all, I can do those exercises anywhere. The stronger I get, the higher I can jump, and the higher I jump allows for more twists and turns while in the air or over hurdles. In my mind, I am already on my way toward reaching at least one of my goals. Plans and dreams go paw in paw, and I have both. I know that I can make it happen if I try hard enough and believe in myself. This is what I am born to do and feel it from the top of my head to the tip of my tail. While saying good bye to my siblings tugs at my heart, leaving the kennel was not a big issue for me since my memories travel with me. I wish that Calm and Calmer could come with me, but a family already has their sights on Calm for adoption. She doesn't have the jumping capabilities that I have or the interest, yet somehow this lack of jumping is acceptable to her new family. Go figure...a dog that doesn't jump. What is attractive about that? Don't they know that artistic jumping is a sign of a highly skilled athlete, and when done correctly, is considered an art form? Have they never seen dogs vault effortlessly into the air after a flying disc, soar incredible lengths from a dock across a huge pool or maneuver through an agility course at the speed of light? I know about those special dogs, and I live in a kennel! At times, I think that pups know a bit more about the world of dog accomplishments than the humans who actually live in the world around them.

Not only am I losing Calm, but also Calmer who is bound for a new home as well as a change in climate. He is

I'm going to miss them so much.

going to leave the bitter cold, snow and chilling winds of the Midwest for a place called Arizona. I'm told that where he is going, the sun shines every day, and there is no threat of the bitter cold we have experienced since birth here in the land of snow, wind and hail. The gravy in his food bowl is that he will get a chance to live his dream. The person who is coming for him is a volunteer puppy raiser from Arizona, and she is not only going to love him to bits but will also prepare him to help others. Palmer is his new name, and it's truly a name befitting a dog destined for service. While I will miss him terribly, I am so happy for him. He is one lucky pup, and maybe, we'll meet again someday. Families have a way of finding each other. He, along with Calm, will always be my family.

Now, I'm just waiting for my new foster family to

They'll be here soon.

arrive at the kennel. My pursuit of world championship glory awaits me as I plunge into new adventures. (*I do have a bit of a flare for the dramatic.*) I have big dreams for my future, and my dreams are going to come true. I'll definitely continue to run, stretch, bend, jump, twist and turn so as to impress the new family in hopes that they share my dreams.

Won't these people be pleasantly surprised and thrilled when I demonstrate my running and jumping skills? Not only are they getting their black, petite, female Labrador Retriever as requested but also a future disc dog, dock diver or agility champion. I can't wait to see their faces when they see me in action as I follow my dreams. They'll see that choosing me is quite a bargain. Just you wait and see...

They're going to love me.

2

Leave It

My new family has just pulled into the driveway of the kennel, and I have to admit that I am a bit nervous about this new, placement situation. I am used to being my own boss, and something tells me that changing locations with a new family won't allow for that type of freedom. My siblings left the kennel yesterday and are off to new adventures, so it's time for me to be on a new journey of my own. While I'm usually quite a confident pup, I find that my nerves are getting the best of me. Evidence of that is the obvious reaction of my hackles not knowing what to do from my neck to my tail. Some are up, and some are down. I don't believe that they even know what to do in this situation. I look like a victim of a bad grooming appointment...perhaps one in a mobile, grooming van when control of equipment isn't at its best. Nevertheless, I'll just work off the nerves by showing this new family what potential I have as an athlete by demonstrating my parallel jumping maneuver. This will render them speechless!

As the two people enter the reception area, they look like a nice, prospective family. The man is quite handsome and has such a gentle look about him. His appearance leads me to believe that I can win him over in a dog bone minute.

The woman, on the other paw, looks a bit more of a challenge. While she has very kind eyes, I get the impression that she just might be the disciplinarian of the two, but I have no facts at the moment to back that up. It's just an uneasy feeling... much like the feeling I get when I eat too much grass, but this particular sensation is making the pads of my paws sweat. I realize that I'm making a snap judgment, but my gut is warning me that I might be entering a "Good Cop/Bad Cop" living arrangement for the next fifteen months. I'm hoping that my nerves are causing my imagination to blur reality because that type of situation would not be an easy one for me. Discipline and free-spirit don't go paw and paw in my world.

Do I win them over with false puppy compliance, a grateful look and perhaps a wag of the tail, or do I attempt to do that with my parallel jumping maneuver? Decision time is finally here. Since first impressions are so important, I go with my gut and continue to carry on with nimble gestures that demonstrate my agility and energy. In simple terms, I defy gravity by jumping up and down in a continuous motion. Within moments, I see that my attempt at winning them over is a lapse in judgment. My amazing jumping isn't even acknowledged, and they don't even make eye contact

Do I look sincere?

with me. Do they not recognize skill and ability in a young, energetic puppy? (*I'm right here folks...catch my eyes on the up jump! Can't you see the excitement glistening in my eyes?*) There's no evident response from them and not even a glint of eye contact...no interest whatsoever. I can already tell that this prospective living arrangement is going to be challenging. How am I ever going to get them to notice me let alone share my special dreams of championship athletic achievement? I'm extremely inventive for my young age, so I know that eventually I'll find a way to win them over to my side.

This is all so confusing.

However, I do need to rest a bit since this jumping up and down is such a drain on my energy. I didn't realize that first impressions could be so exhausting. Now that my ineffective demonstration is over, I sit quietly, and what happens next thoroughly confuses me. The woman with the kind eyes looks down at me and immediately gives me a treat. What kind of game is she playing anyway? I demonstrate my jumping skills, and she doesn't even look at me. I sit quietly, and I'm instantly rewarded with a treat. She's already messing with my mind, and she's definitely good at it because I just don't get it!

Then, something called a collar is placed around my neck with a long bit of rope-like material called a leash attached to it. The woman is talking to me in a soft but confident voice that is throwing me off a bit, and I realize that I'm actually paying attention. If she is my version of the Bad Cop, why is she being so nice to me? Her voice is so soothing that I find myself getting lost in the moment, but then I regroup and face the reality of the situation. She's messing with my mind again, and this collar and leash represent the loss of my freedom. I am no longer a free spirit living recklessly in a kennel, but a puppy who is now making a leashed transition to a new way of life. Suddenly, I realize that I can either comply and make this changeover, or I can be myself and win them over with my athletic capabilities when the time is right. Once again, I'm going with my gut feelings, and they are really going to like my behavioral choice. I guarantee it.

With one last look at the kennel that was my home, I leave it all behind me and take only my memories as my personal traveling companions. Off I go willingly with my new family of sorts. Together, we are Good Cop, Bad Cop and Izzy, the Jumper. I see that they already have a nice, spacious crate arrangement ready for me in the back of their

Who names a car these days?

car called the Blue Baron. I thought it was a strange name, but naming the car was even stranger. Apparently, the Blue Baron replaced their previous car named Sparky 2. That car was involved in a terrible accident coming home from the family's cross-country trip to California with a dog named Kessen. The Blue Baron, the new family car, is a station wagon built for safety and stability but not for racing speed and excitement. That's what I am built for, and that will all come in good time. As I said before, I guarantee it...

3

Let's Go

I took one last look at the kennel that was my home as the Blue Baron angled its way through the winding driveway to the highway. Because my fancy, new crate was facing the back of the car, I was able to look out the rear window and see where I'd been before I knew where I was going. It really seemed a bit backwards to me; but things were going to be different from this point on, so I had better get used to that concept. I suppose if I turned around in the crate and faced the front, I'd see where I was going before we got there. However, riding backwards was a challenge, and today was all about challenges.

As I lost sight of the kennel, I felt a bit light headed since so much had happened in a short period of time. I now had a name, a new foster family and a new direction to my life. My dreams might be on the back food bowl for now, but I was just waiting for the right moment to show my stuff. Then, I'd really be myself and be free to choose the perfect plan for my life.

My only regret was not being able to say good bye to my mother. While I hadn't seen her in weeks, she was the only one who could make my stomach *tingle* with her warmth and strength. Missing that loving feeling would unexpectedly

I sure miss my mom.

wash over me like a wave of sadness, and it seemed somewhat unbearable. But, our mother taught all of us to be strong and independent puppies; and by doing that, we would all make her very proud. Even though her beautiful image was slowly fading from my mind, I'd cling to the memory of her love in my heart. So, I tucked away those sad feelings and looked to the future with hope and confidence.

While there was nothing I could do about her loss, I could make her proud of me by being strong. I truly felt this would, in some way, keep her memory alive for me. Just the thought of that tingling feeling her love and warmth produced would get me through the difficult times. Maybe...just maybe, I'd feel that special *tingle* again when I met someone new and special. I could always hope for that in my new life. I truly believed that if I wished hard enough for something, it would come true. First and foremost, I was definitely a dreamer. New adventures were awaiting me, and even though I was somewhat apprehensive about the future, I felt prepared for what was to come.

Good Cop and Bad Cop took great care to make me comfortable in my new crate. I have to give them points for that, but I was still suspicious of their intentions...especially

Bad Cop's. I had mixed messages from her before when I got nothing for jumping and a treat for sitting still, so I was still leery of her motives. (*One can't be too careful these days.*)

They gave me a few, new toys meant to occupy my time during the ride to my new living space, and I had a great view of the surrounding countryside as we sailed down the highway. Because I had lived in a kennel, everything in this world was new to me. I attempted to take it all in while I gnawed on a bone made of something called rubber that was filled with cheese. I never tasted cheese before, nor did I ever chew a rubber bone. (*I wonder if it's difficult to digest...not that I was making any progress in the gnawing department.*) In any event, I was thoroughly enjoying myself, and thought that perhaps this situation might not be all that terrible. But, I was reserving judgment since it was still early in the journey.

The colors of the countryside were so bright in contrast to the grayish shades found in the kennel. I felt my head swinging from side to side while attempting to take in all of the vivid colors in the trees and shrubs dotting the highway. Good Cop was telling me that the animals grazing peacefully along the fenced meadows were cows, and the rather scruffy, chubby animals crowding the troughs were pigs with their piglets enjoying their afternoon meal. (*From my prospective, they looked like they had a few meals too many.*) The sheep, looking rather disheveled and dingy, just stared at us as we drove by their pens. Each of the farms we passed looked a bit shabby from where I sat, but it wasn't fair for me to judge since I lived in a kennel and didn't know any other way of life until now. I just enjoyed the scenery as we drove through the countryside.

Suddenly I heard a voice from the front seat of the car. "Izzy? Izzy? How are you doing back there?"

It took me a while before I realized that someone was talking to me. I hardly had a chance to get used to my name let alone recognize it when called. What was I supposed to say? Since I didn't know how to communicate with Good Cop and Bad Cop, I just remained silent and continued to gnaw on my new, rubber bone. If they expected me to respond in some way, they sure had pretty high expectations of me! Perhaps I underestimated them and had far more to learn than what I anticipated. I went back to my bone and gnawed in thoughtful silence.

Were they talking to me?

As the farms became fewer and farther between, we came to something called a rest stop. Now, I can't say that I am worldly in any sense of the word, but I do believe this place was misnamed since I didn't get to rest at all. Instead, I was carried out of my crate and placed on the ground in a pet area that had all sorts of unidentified stuff lying around. I had to choose my path wisely for fear that I might just step on something toxic. Worse yet, something might cling to the pads of my paws for the entire rest of the trip. The area was ghastly, and I wasn't quite sure what I was supposed to do. It definitely wasn't a place to run around since it was more of a contaminated, obstacle course. This thing called a leash attached to my so-called collar wasn't even long enough for me to go for a great run around. None the less, I assumed from some of the remnants left on the ground that I was supposed to duplicate the ground cover and, regrettably, do this in front of everyone.

This new world was so confusing not to mention embarrassing. How did any of this fit in with this place being called a rest stop? Nevertheless, I went along with the supposition, and the words of praise from Good Cop when I finished gave my bodily actions credibility. More importantly, the plastic bag he used to remove all remnants of my being there assured me that nothing of mine would be left for others to critique. My presence in that ghastly area would go unnoticed by all who followed in my path.

While I might have been confused with the name of the place since rest was not involved, I did feel a whole lot better after my less than private moment. After retracing my path so as not to step in anything that might linger on my paws for the duration of the ride, I was back in my crate again ready to continue gnawing on my rubber bone.

Off we went to the highway again, and this visit to the rest stop was the first of many adventures that I assumed would occur in my new life. While gradually getting smaller and smaller as we drove away, the rest stop wasn't as intimidating while looking at it through the rear window of the Blue Baron. There's something to be said about facing the back of the car, looking through the rear window and seeing a place slowly shrink in the distance. In my mind, seeing it disappear took away its power to intimidate and renewed my confidence in terms of facing the future. The view from the front of the car would have given me a different perspective of leaving the place but would not have restored my self-confidence. While riding backwards definitely presented some challenges, I was getting the hang of it and learning a lot about myself at the same time.

The scenery changed drastically from farms to buildings located in places called malls. There were so many sights that my head kept shifting from side to side in an effort to see both sides of the road. Huge trucks flashed past us at high speeds. Because I was riding backwards, I could see them coming, and that was a bit scary. Soon, the trucks became fewer, and the living spaces called houses took the place of shops seen in the malls. I couldn't keep track of the houses since there were so many to see, and bright colored flowers and vibrant shrubs lined the streets and driveways. The colors were so beautiful in contrast to the dullness of the highway. Eventually, we pulled into a particular driveway, and I heard Good Cop say that we were now home.

What was a *home*? Since I didn't even know what *home* meant, I just called the new living place a house. I was excited as well as a bit frightened since I really didn't know what I was getting into with this new place. Was I going to be compliant and a bit timid, or was I going to be me and show my new family what I was made of and what I was destined to do?

Right then and there, another major decision was made, and I decided that I was going to give being myself another try. While the first meeting in the kennel didn't have the outcome that I had anticipated, I wasn't going to let that deter me from trying again. I knew exactly what I was going to do when they opened that door to my new way of life... especially if they unclipped this confining thing called a leash.

While Good Cop took me out of my crate and gently placed me on the concrete driveway leading to the house, all I could think of was that my next adventure was about to begin. It was both a thrilling yet intimidating moment, but I was determined to be me. My hackles flew up on my neck in anticipation of the fun and excitement that awaited me on the other side of that back door. I realized that I was more than ready for this because I was a jumping party on paws! This new family was getting a lot more than they bargained for,

I've gotta be me.

and won't they be surprised when I show them how much fun I can be? Let's go and get this party started...

Free At Last

The walk from the car to the back door of the new living place seemed to take forever. The excitement of getting out of the car was only surpassed by the prospect of freedom from this ridiculous rope called a leash. As we got closer to the door, I felt my hackles alerting me to the promise of good times beyond that door, but the trip to that entrance still seemed endless.

Finally, we were at the door, and Good Cop said that I was now going to meet my new brother and sister. A new brother and sister? Was he kidding? First, Good Cop and Bad Cop gave me a name, then a new place to live and now, new siblings. I already had siblings and was definitely not looking for replacements. These people were really taking this fostering business much too seriously. What will they think of next? I have to find a way to be a part of these decisions being made for me. Since I can't speak their language, I have no way to convey my feelings to them as yet. Somehow or some way, I will make my feelings known to them. It's something I just have to do.

Was I overwhelmed due to all of the lifestyle changes in such a short period of time or just immune to what was in store for me beyond that door? In any event, I felt this colossal surge of energy taking charge of my body and realized that nothing was going to stop me from doing what I had to do. Not only was I going to show this new foster family the real me, but I was going to reveal a form of me that I never even knew existed. They were getting that sweet, black, female Labrador Retriever that they originally wanted and so much more in the bargain. My parallel jumping maneuver and running laps would definitely get their attention. Being over stimulated does take on a strange persona, and I was ready to rock and roll!

As I followed Good Cop and Bad Cop into their place, my hackles were in total overdrive. Suddenly, I found myself muzzle to muzzle with two inquiring canines that were sniffing about my body from head to tail. Were these two supposed to be my new siblings? That pseudo-adoption was definitely not going to happen today. Then, miracles of miracles, I felt the leash being unsnapped from my collar, and I was free at last…free from any type of control. As if blasted from a cannon, I took off. While my paws scrambled for traction on the tile floor, I made a break for an opened doorway. In truth, it was not as dramatic as intended because my paws couldn't get much traction on the slippery floor tiles. I looked pretty foolish scrambling and getting nowhere. Nevertheless, persistence is my middle name; and, might I add, one that I gave myself. I eventually gained the traction that I needed and darted through the opened doorway leaving everyone behind in a gust of wind. While I didn't know where I was going, I saw that the kitchen doorway had an opened gate that led to the rest of the house. I took full advantage of my newly acquired speed, shot through the opened gate and raced through any hall or unlocked doorway I could find.

Never knowing that I even had this type of speed before or how it equated to bodily control, I ricocheted off walls, closed doors and bumped furniture while running laps through the house. At one point, my attempt to vault over some elevated food bowls met with disaster when I misjudged the height of the food bowl stand. That type of miscalculation had never happened to me before, but I never traveled at such intense speeds before either. That collision caused the bowls to go crashing down to the floor. The noise was deafening! While I was undoubtedly out of control and a part of me wanted to stop, the adrenalin that seared through my body prevented any end to this disastrous assault on the house.

At one point, I glanced at Good Cop and Bad Cop as I sped around a turn in a carpeted room for the second time, and I do believe their eyes glazed over at the potential of the next fifteen months with me. The two wanna-be siblings just stared in what might have been their expressions of either utter disappointment or total amazement as I zoomed past them. The regal, taller, golden-colored one of the two seemed to frown at my antics, while the petite, shorter, blonde dog appeared intrigued as if she recognized a bit of herself in my antics. Whizzing by them didn't give me much accurate information. While ricocheting off walls and flying through doorways at hair-raising speed demanded a lot of vigor, I felt that my energy level was rapidly decreasing. I was definitely slowing down, and exhaustion was overcoming me.

In my attempt to impress this new family with my athletic skills, speed and agility, I had clearly frightened them with the prospect of spending the next fifteen months with a

They looked dazed.

dog who was capable of chaos and mass destruction. As my energy waned, I ventured slowly through the house in an effort to find them and judge their expressions. I passed floors littered with tossed throw rugs, sofa pillows strewn on the carpet and food bowls turned upside down blocking the hallway. The place was a total mess. My speed was much greater than anticipated given that I undoubtedly didn't recognize my capacity for such mayhem in a short period of time. This chaos was definitely not in my plan to make this family like me or to show them how much I had to offer in terms of a potential, champion athlete. Instead, it was a plan that went very, very wrong.

As I slowly walked to the kitchen area where the family waited in stunned disbelief, I attempted to look somewhat contrite for my outburst of energy and frustration, but I don't think anyone was in a forgiving mood. Good Cop didn't say a word but clicked the leash on me because he thought I might need to take a break outside. I really did need one. A part of me wanted to apologize for my behavior, but I was just too tired. Off we went into the yard, and I was once again controlled by the dreaded leash.

Good Cop is so handsome and very tall.

As I came back into the house and was released from the leash, I noticed the gate from the kitchen to the main part of the house was now closed, and the two resident dogs were on the other side. While restricted to the kitchen area, I looked around and saw special food bowls and some brand new toys. These people were being very nice to me in spite of my atrocious behavior. My intention was to impress them, yet all I did was run rampant through their house, bounced off the walls and doors and created a mess. Perhaps, I just approached my arrival in the wrong manner. Demonstrating my athletic capabilities wasn't such a good idea nor was the resulting destruction.

As I sat in the doorway looking out into the yard, I was suddenly overcome with sadness over the loss of my family

I'm just so overwhelmed.

as well as the carefree life I left behind in the kennel. The disappointment about my first impression on this new family was overwhelming since I thought I could really impress them. How was I ever going to gain their trust after this chaotic display of destruction? Sadness overcame me, and I realized that I learned a very difficult lesson today. Freedom isn't all it is cracked up to be...

5

Under Scrutiny

If ever a pup needed an opportunity for a do-over, this was definitely the day for it. What was meant as a first rate demonstration of my athletic ability quickly turned into an episode of mass destruction. All I wanted to do was show this family the special, athletic skills that I was bringing to their household. How did I know that my enthusiasm would result in utter chaos? My plan was to win them over...not to wreck their house. Visions of the tossed throw rugs, overturned food bowls, scattered sofa pillows and my bouncing off doors and walls, reverberated in my head. I almost expected to be sent back to the kennel for my horrible behavior. If given another chance, my actions will definitely be under intense scrutiny while in this house.

Yet, last night these new people were very kind to me. Perhaps, they saw the sadness and guilt in my eyes over my dreadful demonstration. After the dust settled, and I do mean that literally, order was once again restored to the household. I was given a nice meal, allowed out in the yard and introduced to my very own personal space...a spacious, open concept, wire crate which became my very own kennel. I never had a room of my own before which made this kennel extra special.

I finally have a room of my own.

While settling in, I was once again overcome with loneliness over the loss of my birth mother, my siblings, my old play yard and the former kennel that was my only place to live. My faint whimpers turned to howls that seemed to resonate from some depth of emotion that I had never felt before. Unable to stop, I continued to howl taking only infrequent gasps of air. Because of the open concept of the new kennel, my grief was public, and I so longed for some privacy while in the depth of my sadness. I know that sounds very dramatic, but I was one, hurting puppy.

Good Cop sought peace and quiet at the other end of the house, and the two dogs followed in quick succession. The noise was much too ear piercing for them. Bad Cop sat silently in the shadows from across the room. As if she felt my pain and need for privacy, she ever so gently partially covered my kennel with a sheet. That thoughtful act of kindness gave me a momentary *tingle* in my stomach similar to what I felt for my birth mother's love...only this *tingle* was just a faint flutter in the pit of my stomach. Still, it gave me some small bit of comfort in my time of need. With the sheet covering my new kennel, my grief was now somewhat private. My howling continued on and off for most of the night in spite of the faint sounds of calming music meant especially for pups who were stressed. I was certainly stressed, but the music wasn't helping me at all. Exhaustion finally overcame me, and I was able to sleep.

In the midst of this inner turmoil and outward expressions of my sadness, I was most grateful for Bad Cop's kindness and realized that I could no longer call her by that name. It just didn't seem right anymore...not after her tenderness shown to me at such a low point in my life and especially after the destruction I caused during my arrival. I'd really have to think of some appropriate name for her, but I also had to figure out how to get back into the good graces of all the members of the household.

Even though exhausted from my vocal expressions of sadness throughout the night, I knew that I was capable of winning them over. I needed a plan...a good plan that didn't involve jumping, vaulting, racing through the house or ricocheting off doors and walls. My athletic goals and dreams would have to be on the back burner of the food bowl for now because I had to get the humans to like me. Since I couldn't communicate with them in their own language, I had to start with my only source of communication. That would definitely mean getting to know the two dogs already living here in the house.

First of all, I had to convince those two canines of my sincerity, and that might not be so easy due to my energetic

I'm really very lovable.

entrance to their house last night. But, today was a new day, and anything was pawsable. I could be charming and especially charming if I thought it might help me out of a difficult situation. While my intentions were good, that sure sounded somewhat shallow...even for me, but desperate situations called for desperate measures. Now, I just had to make a plan for them to like me, and that wouldn't be easy since my plans so far hadn't even been close to being successful. This one had to work in order to be accepted by the members of the household, and that goal was of the utmost importance to me. My dreams of athletic glory would have to be put on hold for now. "Operation Like Me" was up and running, and I was determined to attain that goal.

Since the plan was in the very early stages of development, I felt a nap would help me get my thoughts together. Who was I kidding? I didn't have a clue as to how to even begin. Even giving it an appropriate name was exhausting, so sleep was my only escape from reality. Before I was lost in dream land, I heard the two resident dogs ambling over to the kitchen gate. The larger one...the slim, regal-looking Golden Retriever/Labrador Retriever mix

I don't think they like me.

entered the hall as if he were the grand master of a holiday parade. As he looked down at me through the fence rails, his piercing eyes seemed to scrutinize me in a way that made me shrink a bit in my own skin. He was definitely the elder and alpha of the household, canine pack. His white, masked face showed not only his age but gave him a look of grandeur that highlighted his high ranking status. He definitely would be the tough one of the two to win over. "Operation Like Me" was definitely not going to be an easy accomplishment with this dude...no disrespect intended.

The other canine was a beautiful, blonde Labrador Retriever/Golden Retriever mix, but she was much shorter in stature than the other dog. Her position behind the elder dog confirmed her recognition of his status. She did, however, have a sparkle of mischief in her brown eyes that almost seemed to convey the possibility of friendship between us. I wondered if their perceptions of me were as decisive as mine of them. Nevertheless, my path of destruction left in last night's assault on the house just might have distorted their opinions of me to a great extent. I really had a tough job ahead of me if my plan were to work.

I cautiously approached the gate. Since I wasn't able to give an appropriate sniff, out of respect to the elder, I gave one of my finest play bows. Needless to say, he did not return the bow. Instead, he positioned himself on the floor, introduced himself as Kessen, the pack leader of the house, and began a litany of house rules. Midway between some of his rules and regulations, I attempted unsuccessfully to suppress a yawn. This did not please Kessen at all. Insulted by this unintentional rudeness on my part, Kessen got up, gave me a look of disappointment and walked away. I guess that attempt to get him to like me didn't work either, but I honestly couldn't help yawning. After all, I had howled most of the night, and a growing pup needs rest. (*There I go making excuses again.*)

I suddenly realized that getting everyone to like me was going to be a tough gig, and getting Kessen's acceptance was even more difficult after our first muzzle to muzzle encounter. Back home in my former kennel, life was so much easier because I didn't have rules and regulations. In this place, I ate when food was put in front of me, played when allowed in the yard on a tether because I could still fit through the fence rails and slept when the lights were turned off at night. This new living situation was just so rigid and, at times, confusing as well.

While I might have lost my initial chance with Kessen, I thought that I might still have a chance with the other dog. I called her Blondie because of her flaxen coat. While calling her that wasn't politically correct, I meant no disrespect. Since I hadn't been formally introduced, I just went with my eyes and not my brain. She was gorgeous, and those brown eyes reminded me of dark chocolate…the kind that dogs aren't supposed to eat. There was definitely mischief in those eyes. While that fact alone might be a warning of what was to come, I never let warnings get in my way before, so why start now?

As she approached the gate, I once again gave a most respectful play bow to her. Believe it or not, she not only returned the bow but spun around three times and barked once. Was that some sort of ritualistic greeting for newcomers in the house? I wasn't sure, but I accepted it as a friendly gesture. She told me that her name was Brightie, short for Brighton. Both she and Kessen were not only permanent residents of the household but were also co-captains of the Socialization Squad. Their job was to work with newcomers and teach them to be respectful and happy family members of the household. She seemed very sincere about her dedication to her position. I have to tell you, I had never heard of anything like that before. It was an interesting concept, but I

could think of some disadvantages to that process…at least from my own, personal point of view. However, who am I to challenge the system? I needed these dogs to like me so I had to be on my very best behavior.

They work together as a team.

Most confusing was that I didn't even know what my best behavior was! I certainly hadn't shown it so far in this relocation experience, and behaviors in my former kennel were never discussed…other than that "she's a bit of a jumper" remark that was shared when the new family came to pick me up. As a result, I'm really in a foreign dog park with this best behavior concept. Trial and error will have to be my guide, and I already had a head start in the process…error being the operative word. It was safe to say that last night's incident was definitely not an example of best behavior. At the very least, I had a negative starting point towards that goal. My only direction was up!

Brightie also let it slip that she, herself, was a bit of a mischief-maker. Apparently, my escapades of the night before were not as devastating to her as to the others in the house.

That fact alone led me to believe that we were going to be good friends. After all, mischief-making is proving to be one of my greatest talents. If that talent were shared by even one of the canines in this household, perhaps I now had an ally for attaining my goal of having everyone like me.

Be mindful that all of my previous plans had not even

Will you help me?

come close to being successful. I would need all the help I could get not only in formulating the "Operation Like Me" plan but in its implementation in the days to come. With Brightie's help, I had a genuine chance at succeeding. Only time would tell, and time was definitely on my side...

Taking a Break

After my early morning, semi-successful meeting with the elder named Kessen and the blonde beauty named Brightie, I was almost dreading seeing Good Cop and Bad Cop for the first time that day. Last night, Good Cop found peace and quiet at the other end of the house with Kessen and Brightie, but Bad Cop stayed at a distance in the room while I wailed away the night with shrieks and howls. What must she think of me? I shuddered at the mere thought of her first impression of me. I felt that I'd get a break with Good Cop, but Bad Cop was one tough bone to chew.

They eventually came into the kitchen, and I attempted to give them not only an apologetic look, but a sitting position that demonstrated my regret over the actions of the previous day. Instead of some form of reprimand, they greeted me happily with "Good morning, Izzy. Today is a new day, and new days are meant for good times." They actually acted like nothing happened.

Did they not remember the chaos of last night? Were they both messing with my mind today? Is this another one of those mind games initiated by Bad Cop? It really sounded like something that would come directly from her since mind-messing seemed to be her specialty. Now I was very confused.

I expected some form of reprimand...even a trip to the post office to send me back to the kennels, but kindness wasn't even in the expectations of today's interaction with the humans. These are real curve balls in the food bowl of life, and I was in for a much greater challenge than expected. For once, I felt that I was at a disadvantage in the mind game department, and for me, that was quite an admission. Perhaps I was not as smart as I thought, and how was that even possible? Such a crushing blow to my ego! Maybe taking a break from my dream of athletic glory and focusing on being accepted into this household was the best idea of the day.

Don't they remember what I did?

The early morning really went quite well. I was fed, taken out for a while in the yard and even had some time to run around a bit. I felt a lot better after eating and figured that since the humans of the house were willing to forgive my atrocious behavior of the night before, then I would attempt to make it up to them in terms of changes in my behavior. I sure couldn't guarantee total, good behavior, but I would make every effort to be better. They just weren't ready for another demonstration of my athletic talents, and taking a break from that dream was the best possible move at this point in time.

While "Operation Like Me" remained a priority, I felt that I still needed to come up with new names for these people who not only took me in but seemed to keep me after my escapades of the night before. Anyone else might have shipped me back to the kennels as soon the sun came up, but these people were giving me another chance. While I might not have made a very good impression on them yesterday, I did have fifteen months with them to change their minds.

I also wondered if that time frame gave them the creeps. After all, their eyes did glaze over while I assaulted their house, and fifteen months with a whirling bundle of energy may seem like some form of penance to them. It was hard to tell since today seemed to be a day of forgiveness. I'll just have to take one day at a time since this new living arrangement was much more difficult than living in a kennel, and that's a fact.

Aside from the possible disturbing notion of having me around for the next fifteen months, I also had to consider an even greater task than having them like me. Following my dreams had to wait while I thought about new names for these humans. Bad Cop stayed in the shadows last night amidst my howling and gave me the greatest gift of kindness by placing a sheet over my kennel...giving me privacy for my sadness. She didn't have to do that but recognized my need for it. I couldn't keep calling her Bad Cop after that sincere gift to me. It just wasn't right even though I knew that she was still good at mind-messing. In addition to that, I did feel a slight *tingle* when she did that for me, and that *tingle* was so reminiscent of my mother's love. Even if Bad Cop's *tingle* were just a momentary flutter, I just wasn't prepared to call her mom right now, and maybe I never would be. I just didn't have the right name for her as yet, and finding a perfect name would take some time. So, I decided to just call her B.C. for now. It was just an interim name, but definitely a step up from Bad Cop. While on the other paw, what was I going to call Good Cop? I couldn't just give B.C. a new name and not think about him. Even though he fled to the other side of the house last night to avoid my shrieking, he still deserved a less formal name than Good Cop. He had always been kind and

A nap would help.

gentle with me from the first time we met. He, too, deserved a perfect name, but that would also take some serious thought. Until I found the right one, I'd just refer to him as G.C. It was certainly not as official as Good Cop, but it was the best I could come up with on short notice.

Thinking of better names was certainly more of a challenge than I anticipated. After I had more sleep, I'd have better results since naps were so mentally stimulating. So off I went to my kennel to catch some long overdue sleep. While Both B.C. and G.C were certainly not the most creative names, they would have to do for now...

7

Rise To The Occasion

A week had passed since my chaotic arrival, and conditions in the household had settled down a bit. Putting my athletic ambitions on hold while I concentrated on "Operation Like Me" was definitely the right thing to do. Since I was not bouncing off doors and walls on a daily basis, B.C. and G.C. seemed to smile a lot more when they came into my kitchen area. I called it my kitchen area because most of my time was spent in that room in addition to my kennel. I heard mention that the kitchen was my special place because I wasn't fully housebroken, but I wasn't sure what that meant. I came pretty close to breaking the house when I first arrived, but I don't think that's what B.C. and G.C. meant when they talked about housebreaking. I believed it had something to do with bodily functions, and I'm certainly no expert on that. After all, I spent my early months in a kennel and didn't have any restrictions in terms of when and where housebreaking rules applied. But, in this house, the kitchen area was the closest route to the dog run and was the logical place for me to stay.

Settling into a daily routine had helped as well, but I was told that today was a special day since I would be starting school...something called Puppy Kindergarten. I didn't know what that was either, but it must be important because B.C. had a bag all packed with treats, plastic bags, water, the dreaded leash and a special type of covering called a cape. I'm not sure what the cape was for, but B.C. had me wear it each day for a little while. It had patches on it with some writing, but I didn't know what it said. Maybe it had to do with B.C. and G.C.'s goal for me as a future assistance dog. One thing was very

Today is a special day.

clear...my not knowing how to read put me at a distinct disadvantage. I had so many things to learn in this new environment. Because my daily routine was very different from my kennel days, most days were filled with new experiences and opportunities for learning. I was definitely a busy pup these days!

I gave a friendly tail wag to Kessen and Brightie as B.C. and I left for my first day of school. Kessen gave a slight nod of acknowledgement, and Brightie just spun around three times and barked. She did that a lot, and I'm not sure why it was important to her since that spinning just made me dizzy. Apparently, it didn't affect her since she continued to do it. B.C. told Brightie that she wasn't the best mentor for me, but Brightie didn't care. (*I liked Brightie's nonchalant attitude.*) I didn't know what being a mentor meant either, but I enjoyed seeing the mischievous glint in Brightie's eyes when she did her spin routine. I believed that in time, we definitely would be the best of friends; but for now, I was just trying to stay out of trouble. I feared that joining Brightie's escapades was a clear-cut trip down the rocky road to mischief...a trip that I definitely had to avoid.

I was once again crated in the back of the Blue Baron. As it glided through the streets and highways, I actually enjoyed the backward scenery that came with riding in that section. After driving for a while, we ended up in what was called an industrial area. Huge buildings surrounded by fencing lined the road. Once the car was parked, the prospect of a new adventure excited me. I was careful to sit nicely while B.C. opened the door of the crate and put the signature cape on me. I had to keep reminding myself of "Operation Like Me" and how important it was for me to behave. It was a lot tougher than I thought, but I was determined to be successful and to rise to the occasion. I wasn't actually sure what "rise to the occasion" meant, but B.C. made it a point to say that it was her expectation regarding my behavior. I gathered that I was to conduct myself in an orderly manner. What were the odds of that happening in the midst of a new and exciting experience? There was a lot of pressure on me for wise choices and good behavior. After all, I was just a puppy, and by nature, puppies do goofy things. It was like walking on a tight rope...one wrong step and game over!

When we entered the waiting room of this huge building, I was met with an explosion of sounds...all sorts of barking, howling and whining going on in the next room. This was definitely going to be fun, and perhaps behaving myself wasn't a reasonable expectation for this adventure. My hackles were on full alert for this new and exciting venture into the unknown.

As the door opened to the larger room, I lunged forward in an attempt to pull my way through the doorway only to be stopped quickly by the leash going taut. B.C. stood perfectly still while I pulled, lunged, jumped, whined, sat and finally realized that we weren't going anywhere. I couldn't figure out why B.C. was stopping me. What was the purpose of heading to the door if we weren't going to go in? It just didn't make sense to me, so I reluctantly came back to her side to find out what was going on.

Once settled, we were on our way again to what I playfully named the Fun Room. Lunging forward again was met with the same, taut leash, and I suddenly suspected that B.C. was messing with my head again. I didn't think that we were meant to go into that room at all because every time I bolted for the door, I was stopped. However, I was secretly making some headway. Each time that happened, we got a little closer to the doorway. After numerous foiled attempts at getting to the Fun Room my way, I decided to do it B.C.'s way. I grudgingly walked into the room by her side and saw by B.C.'s expression that I did, indeed, rise to the occasion. Now, I knew what her words meant. It was all about what was considered good behavior. Evidently, my getting into the room her way made that happen. It was her way or no way! Nevertheless, let me be clear about this…even though I gave in to her method of entering a room, I also accomplished my goal because I was now exactly where I wanted to be...in the Fun Room. Let the learning games begin!

The huge, training room was an awesome sight to behold. Puppies were pulling, lunging and barking all over the place. Handlers were being dragged into the room by puppies straining at their leashes. Once seated, the handlers attempted to calm the active pups. Everywhere I looked, there was excitement, but a sudden hush came over the room when this petite woman with flaming red hair entered and walked to the center of the room. She introduced herself as our instructor for the class and welcomed us to Puppy Kindergarten. The kindness in her eyes as well as her confident tone of voice were, at the same time, calming yet intimidating to all of us. Her name was Joy, and just as her name implied along with her tone of voice, enthusiasm and welcoming demeanor, there was a promise of happiness and excitement in the weeks to come.

Joy also had two special assistants named Nivin and Rachel who helped with the class. Just seeing them in action in this first class gave hints as to what fun we were to have with them in the weeks to come. Their personalities complemented each other in that Nivin seemed to be more outgoing and gregarious, while Rachel had a quiet and calm manner. I could tell that all the pups in the class would be responsive to their directions, and we were going to have a treat bowl full of fun!

Nivin and Rachel were also going to demonstrate various training procedures during the classes after Joy explained what to do and how to do the various training techniques. Each of us would get a chance to be in demonstrations as demo-dogs with these amazing assistants. The real icing on the dog biscuit came when they mentioned using peanut butter and pieces of dried liver. There's nothing closer to a pup's heart than peanut butter and dried liver! The class sounded better and better with each passing moment, and it was apparent that Puppy Kindergarten was just a party waiting to happen. I couldn't wait for the class to begin.

As the handlers introduced themselves and their dogs, I surveyed the room and saw quite a variety of pups in the class. There were nine pups in all, and each was raring to go except for the Bull Dog pup named Oscar...who just looked exhausted. He had a sweet face surrounded by numerous folds, and his ears were dark brown in contrast to his full, white face. He wasn't too enthusiastic about being here and curled up in nest-like fashion next to his handler's chair. I was the only black Labrador Retriever in the class as well as the only pup wearing a cape. Was wearing the cape meant to be something special, or was it an identification of some type of abnormality? My not knowing the cape's significance was just another disadvantage of being a non-reader.

On my right was a petite, snow-white Poodle named Precious who attempted to roll her eyes in disgust when her handler told us her name. The expression on her face not only showed her dislike of her given name, but it also had a hint of mischief that promised some fun in the weeks to come. On my left was a Siberian Husky named Frank. Because he had blue eyes, his handler named him for someone referred to as

Old Blue Eyes. It was confusing to me since I never heard of anyone having that name, but Frank seemed okay with it.

The others in the group consisted of a fawn-colored Boxer named Lucy who was quite delicate looking with her long legs and thin, athletic body. Across the room was a timid, rust-colored Golden Retriever named Penny whose large, almond eyes slowly surveyed the room while a huge, coal-black Great Dane named Nathan hovered over the rest of us in terms of height. Next to Nathan was the most diminutive pup in the class. She was a sable-colored Italian Greyhound named Panini who visually looked like the size of Nathan's head. While such a size difference might have been intimidating to some pups, Panini's aristocratic look and confident manner were in themselves intimidating. In fact, she looked quite comfortable sitting next to such a giant. Being a sighthound by nature gave her the edge as she scanned the room with an intense gaze. The high-spirited, yellow Labrador Retriever named Jake was the final pup on the class roster. We were certainly quite an unusual assortment of pups. With the exception of Oscar, we were all ready to get this party started.

We were quite the unique group. While we had our differences in terms of size, color and temperament, we definitely had one thing in common: pulling on the leash. We were united in that effort as if strangling ourselves was an intentional goal on our parts. As students in Puppy Kindergarten, we presented a great challenge not only to our handlers but also to the expert instructor and her well-qualified assistants.

Our excitement was short lived in that we actually spent some time on learning. Time was spent on responding to our names, sitting on command, inappropriate jumping (*which seemed futile when looking at our group*) and soft mouthing (*which also seemed ridiculous to me since anything worth eating should be done with gusto*). We also learned something called "got-cha" which was a non-threatening technique for grabbing the collar of a dog to either restrain or control. Once again, I learned something new since I thought "got-cha" was what one said after a treat or fly was caught in mid-air! In my defense, I did spend my early months in a kennel.

I know this stuff.

I already knew my new name and how to sit correctly although I didn't see the purpose in sitting since it just wasted time. Furthermore, I considered jumping to be an athletic skill rather than an unsightly behavior. In fact, I already had conflicting issues with this class curriculum. However, I reminded myself of B.C.'s instructions to "rise to the occasion" as well as my "Operation Like Me" plan. I would go along with the program for as long as I could, but no guarantees were etched into the treat bowl of puppy promises.

While we all made various attempts at some of the exercises, the gravy in the dog bowl came toward the end of the class. We were going to have a special exercise in socialization that involved play time with each other. Joy made sure that we were all pretty well matched in size and demeanor, but the Husky and the Great Dane would play in the other room due to their size. B.C. took off my cape since I wasn't allowed to play when wearing it and held my collar while waiting for the signal to play.

The magic moment came as the leashes were removed, release words were given, and we were set free to play. I immediately paired up with the Boxer who seemed to do these ballerina-like jumps over my twisting and turning body. She was incredible...go Lucy go! Panini raced ahead of all of us and led the pack as we sprinted our way around the huge room. Running at top speed, Jake, the other Labrador Retriever in the class, matched my pace. Nevertheless, none of us could match Panini's speed. Precious, the Poodle, caught up with us as we ended up rolling around in a ball of fun and excitement. Penny, the Golden Retriever, found a safe place under a chair since our antics seemed to frighten her. Oscar, the Bull Dog, never did move from his spot by his handler. In fact, I don't think he moved at all during the entire class. Nevertheless, Lucy, Panini, Jake, Precious and I had the time of our lives. This thing called socialization was a hackle's delight, a puppy's dream come true and definitely something to look forward to in the next class.

Frank and Nathan joined us at the end of the class following their socialization time, and there should have been a contest for whose tongue was hanging the closest to the ground following the frolicking. I do believe that Nathan would have won since his tongue was considerably longer than all of ours combined. Puppy Kindergarten was so much fun, and our exhaustion was proof of that. All the pups would sleep well tonight, and everyone knew that a tired pup was a good pup.

I really looked forward to my next lesson, and while I was exhausted from the experience, I couldn't wait to tell Kessen and Brightie about the fun I had in class. Helicopter tail wags to B.C. for enrolling me in this awesome class. As we got ready to leave the Fun Room, I couldn't help but throw caution to the wind, forget about "Operation Like Me" and show my appreciation to Joy, Nivin, Rachel, B.C. and all of my classmates by demonstrating my version of the Lab *zooms* for them.

For those of you who don't know what those are, they are impulsive expressions of excitement demonstrated by a dog running at full speed around a room, an enclosure or any space. Often referred to as the *goofies*, the *crazies* or the *zooms*, they are actions that require four distinct elements: hugging the ground while running at full speed, keeping the head down, tucking the tail and, to top it off, the action must be unexpected. The element of surprise is essential to a good *zoom*!

As I took off in full *zoom* mode, the force of my startling behavior jerked the leash from B.C.'s hands. As I ran around the room, I was in my glory reveling in the events of the class while the leash took flight behind me due to my extreme speed. I was like a stealth bomber...my shiny, black coat hugged the floor while I circled the room with my leash flying high in the air behind me. As the other pups in the class looked on in awe of my behavior, I did catch a glimpse of B.C.'s expression as I flew by her for the second time. It certainly wasn't an expression of pride, but I just couldn't help myself. The preceding week of "Operation Like Me" had taken its toll in terms of self-control, and I was just vulnerable to one such expression of freedom. The *zoom* demon had taken control of me, and I was powerless to stop.

After about four turns around the room, up the stairs, across the stage and back down again, I finally slowed down and meandered toward B.C. attempting to look contrite, but in truth, not even coming close to being successful. She quietly took hold of the leash, said nothing to me and led me from the class. As I looked back at my classmates, I caught a glimpse of an appreciative wink from Lucy as well as looks of admiration from Precious, Jake, Panini, Nathan, Frank and even Penny who came out from under her chair during my exhibition. Oscar, on the other paw, remained asleep by his handler's chair and missed the entire event.

Even though I knew that there would be consequences for my behavior, I had the following week to plan for the next class and to gain B.C.'s forgiveness. Did I rise to the occasion in terms of good behavior as B.C. wanted? In spite of my earlier valiant efforts, sadly, I did not...

Meet And Greet

Following my demonstration of the *zooms*, the ride home from Puppy Kindergarten was rather silent. In spite of that, I just couldn't wait to tell Kessen and Brightie all about my experience. The class was such a special event, and there were five more classes to attend with more opportunities for fun and excitement...especially the play time. I definitely had to work on my self-control in terms of *zooming*, but I didn't have to worry about that right now.

Kessen was a bit dismissive when I told him about my experience since he thought that my behavior was totally disrespectful to the group, but Brightie was on the edge of her haunches while I explained the events. She was especially interested in what led to my getting the *zooms* as well as the reaction of my classmates. She knew what the humans would think about them but was eager to hear about the pups' response. As anticipated, she was thrilled that I demonstrated my enjoyment of the class with an extreme version of *zooming* and that the pups in the group appreciated it. Brightie was definitely my soul mate.

Given that B.C. and G.C. hadn't shipped me back to the kennel for my intermittent, reckless behavior, both Kessen and Brightie had resigned themselves to my staying in the sorority house. Both thought it was time for me to have a meet and greet with some of the dogs in the neighborhood. The yard was the perfect place for that to happen because the important dogs lived next door on both sides of the house. This was going to be fun, and I was eager to meet the neighbors.

Since I had grown some and my head was too large to fit through the fence rails, I had been allowed to run freely in the huge yard and had a glorious time running back and forth through the snow-covered shrubbery. I was told that the tall bushes framing the north end of the yard were called Red Twig Dogwoods and, in my opinion, were the perfect place to play hide and seek. Although they were red and had twigs of all sizes and shapes, I don't understand why they were called dogwoods since they don't come close to resembling woods. Where were the leaves, tree trunks and branches? They didn't have dogs in them either since I foolishly looked for the dogs among the twigs. In my defense once again, I lived in a kennel and wasn't familiar with the ways of the world.

The rest of the yard had all sorts of snow-laden bushes, shrubs and trees. I enjoyed running along the fence line between the fence and the dogwoods, and then making a swift turn under the Blue Spruce trees and around the Burning Bushes. That was another strange name for bushes since they weren't close to being on fire and looked more like a bunch of twigs at this time of the year. From time to time, the language of the human world was just too baffling. Nevertheless, I enjoyed the huge enclosure, the obstacles in the forms of foliage as well as the ability to zigzag my way through the open spaces of the yard. My imagination conjured up all sorts of enemies lurking in the snow drifts, the bushes and under the trees. I even practiced my parallel jumps that were high enough to see the other side of the fence. Spinning and twirling added to the delight of the yard experience. Life was good.

I hadn't met any other dogs in the neighborhood, but apparently Kessen and Brightie now felt that I was ready for those introductions. The first time we all ran out into the yard together was very chaotic. Kessen took the lead while carrying a large ring toy in his mouth. Then, Brightie followed with a squeak-ball in her mouth, and I lurked closely behind with a rather large twig in my mouth that I had found on

Kessen loved that toy.

my way out of the house. Our combined speed was intense at first but of short duration. Kessen was the first to stop and rest while hovering over his precious toy. I was instructed by Brightie that under no circumstances was I to touch Kessen's ring toy. At first I thought that she was kidding, but the look in her eyes told me otherwise; so I didn't even approach him. Brightie left the formation to run around in the open spaces with her ball, and I just bolted in between bushes and trees while carrying that dried twig. When Kessen got bored with his ring toy, he called me over to the north side of the fence line where a very handsome Golden Retriever stood silently on the other side.

He's so very wise.

This awesome-looking dog was named Sammy and was the neighborhood sage and resident historian. His long, golden coat glistened in the sunlight, and his face not only revealed the mask of his age but one of wisdom. For years, Sammy was the official source of all neighborhood information. Well respected for his ability to remember past occurrences in the vicinity, Sammy was, indeed, a dog who was worth knowing. He didn't seem to be surprised by my presence since he was used to a variety of pups coming and going in our yard and told me that he had been watching me for quite a while through the fence rails. He thought I had potential in terms of being a successful member of the sorority house and was grateful that I demonstrated some form of common sense in terms of the yard experience. While I wasn't sure what he meant by that, he went on to tell me that when Kessen was a pup, he got his head stuck between the fence rails when he rushed the fence without properly judging his speed and ability to stop. My first thought was to laugh, but I knew Kessen was positioned right behind me. We were already making headway in the friend department, so I repressed that response and just listened attentively to Sammy's tales from the past.

Sammy was also anxious to tell me that when Kessen was just a pup, he actually thought that the baby pool was a huge, water bowl. Now, my reaction to that bit of information was almost too much to suppress, so I hid my laughter with a momentary, made-up coughing spell. Much to my chagrin, it didn't go unnoticed by Kessen, but in my defense, that story was really funny.

It was interesting that Kessen represented himself as this household dignitary, yet he had done some ridiculous

Sammy had great stories.

things as a pup. While this knowledge gave me some surprising insights into Kessen's early days, it also restored my faith in the foibles of puppyhood. Way to go, Kessen!

Obviously, this meet and greet wasn't going as well as Kessen planned since Sammy was telling tales of his goofiness as a pup. After all, Kessen had a reputation to maintain as head of the sorority house, so he was eager to move on to the next introduction.

Sammy, in his astuteness as the neighborhood sage, just looked at me and said..."Wisdom comes with age, and there is definitely hope for you yet. Nevertheless, don't run between the fence line and the dogwoods...those twigs will poke your eyes out!" With that bit of insight, he turned and sauntered back to his house.

Sammy is unquestionably an awesome dog who possesses great wisdom and is willing to share it with others. To be honest, I never thought about the possibility of poking my eyes out while running along the fence line until Sammy mentioned it. Those twigs sticking out at all angles never posed a threat until now. I was certainly glad that Kessen introduced us and meeting Sammy might have just saved my vision. Kessen wasn't looking all that pompous after Sammy spilled the kibble on his past puppy behaviors, but he had more introductions to make and once again assumed his air of superiority.

As if given a cue, running around the outside perimeter of the fence line was this huge, chocolate-colored Labrador Retriever named Finnegan. His spectacular muscles glistened in the sunlight while his eyes sparkled with mischief as he raced back and forth. Kessen referred to him as the official neighborhood Welcome

Finnegan worked out a lot.

Wagon all rolled into one, fine specimen of a canine.

Finnegan lived life to the fullest and was the envy of all dogs forced into compliance by either above or below ground fencing. He was the hiker, the camper, the swimmer and the hunter of all things real and imagined. While his owners cross country skied along the Prairie Path in the forest preserve, Finnegan was free to jump in and out of huge snow drifts while other dogs just imagined that carefree experience. He was the neighborhood's free spirit and nothing stood in his way of a good time.

On the other paw, he had a serious side in that one of his jobs was to greet the individuals who walked along the sidewalk as they passed his driveway. He would silently rest in the comfort of his garage until a walker came by, and then he would greet them happily with barks of joy as they passed. He missed no one and was serious about his commitment to making the walkers feel welcome as they went by his house. I could tell that he really took great pride in his job.

Finnegan's enthusiasm was contagious, and his athletic build was proof of his dedication to good health, strength and canine fitness. He was also known as the neighborhood Dog's Dog. Even though he was anxious to meet me, he was in a bit of a hurry and didn't stop to chat.

"Catch you later, Toots! I just caught a fresh scent that I can't resist." With that, he was off speeding through yards with his nose close to the ground in hot pursuit of some sort of trophy to take home to the family.

That dog just called me Toots! I was appalled at the arrogance of that canine clown, but Brightie just laughed and explained to me that the neighborhood Dog's Dog must like me since he gave me a special name, and special privileges came with the Dog's Dog title. Brightie just encouraged me to calm down and enjoy the view of Finnegan running through the yards. I had to admit that he certainly was a great example of canine fitness…especially when he was sprinting at full speed. He must work out a lot!

Kessen just rolled his eyes as he attempted to regain control of his meet and greet. Nothing was going quite the way he planned, and we still had another dog to meet. As we walked to the other side of the yard, Kessen instructed me to follow him to the front of the house. We managed to plow through the mounds of snow that seemed to cover everything and stopped at the property line.

In the front yard of the house next door, I spotted a huge statue situated in the snow. But, this statue wasn't a gray-colored one that was typically seen on some front lawns and in yards. This one was not only enormous, but it had colorful markings on its shape. Judging by the size, it looked to me more like a monument. As I looked closer, I saw that it was a figure of a large dog gracing the middle of the front, snow-covered lawn.

That statue is huge!

Without any warning whatsoever, the statue turned his head

and stared at us. That action not only startled me but awakened my hackles from tip to tail. What kind of statue moved like that?

Kessen just laughed at my sudden response and told me to follow him to the statue. As we got closer, I saw that the figure wasn't a statue at all. It was actually a magnificent-looking canine who had burrowed himself into a snow mound on the front lawn of his house. Then, I was introduced to Kaiser, the Bernese Mountain Dog, who was the official resident sentinel of the front lawns. In addition to his size, his markings were superb with their

He's such a magnificent dog!

unique combinations of black, white and rust covering his face and body. Yet, those penetrating, dark brown eyes that seemed to follow movement even though his head didn't move were his most significant assets. Seeing his eyes shift without any movement of his head was both an eerie and intimidating experience. In an effort to preserve the safety of the front lawns and alert the dogs in residence to any sort of danger, Kaiser maintained his position on a daily basis in all sorts of weather without ever taking a day off. Here was a dog who took his job seriously.

Kessen introduced me as the newest member of the sorority house. In spite of Kaiser's size, he gracefully assumed a sitting position in order to greet me appropriately. Apparently, he had seen me from time to time getting in and out of the car and told me that he was happy to finally make my acquaintance. After welcoming me to the neighborhood, he once again resumed his position as sentinel in the snow. He was a dog of few words but definitely a dog with class.

While Kessen's plans for the neighborhood meet and greet didn't go entirely as planned, he was definitely pleased

All's well that ends well.

that I was able to meet the key players in the area. His pride in knowing them was evident. Although the dogs had unique differences, which to me made them extremely interesting, they also had significant jobs in the neighborhood that they took quite seriously. They were invaluable assets to their canine community, and I was honored to meet them. Perhaps one day I would have a significant job somewhere…one that would make Kessen as proud of me as he was of his friends. It was certainly something to consider…

9

Quiet Rebellion

After Puppy Kindergarten classes ended, I entered the next level of obedience training called Puppy Continuing. Some of my friends from Puppy Kindergarten were in the class, and I enjoyed catching up with their news. Nathan, the Great Dane, had gotten even bigger than imagined. Jake, the blonde Labrador Retriever, was as frisky as ever while Precious, the Poodle, sporting a rather unusual haircut, didn't look at all pleased with her new trim. The Golden Retriever named Penny was surprisingly animated as Lucy, the sleek and slim Boxer, bounced around next to me throughout most of the class. Frank, the blue-eyed Husky, the Italian Greyhound named Panini and Oscar, the Bull Dog, were not in our class. They probably learned enough in Puppy Kindergarten to be good pets and didn't need to continue.

Joy was our instructor again, but she assumed a more serious approach to this level of learning. Nivin and Rachel were once again the fun-for-all assistants and continued to randomly select us for demonstrations. The classes were fun, but the extreme disappointment was that we no longer played with each other at the end of the sessions. The announcement was made that we were too old to play in class since we were on the path to obedience at its highest level. Seriously? In my opinion, pups were never too old to play, but I wasn't in charge. The *zooms* became a bit of my signature finale at the end of each class. Every once in a while, I even interjected that activity during the class itself...much to the chagrin of B.C. When I did that, she just shook her head, assumed an unyielding stance which forced me to stop, and then just led me back to our assigned area. I guess one can take the pup out of the *zoom* but can't take the *zoom* out of the pup! It was, after all, my signature move, and I took great pride in my ability to be spontaneous with it.

I must admit that this no-play format as part of the curriculum brushed my coat the wrong way. While we were waiting for our third session to begin, I wondered if we might change that policy. What if all the pups just assumed a down position as a silent protest and refused to move until the instructor changed the format to include play time? It sounded like a reasonable request, and such a tactic seemed to me to be a stroke of genius. Why didn't I think of it sooner? The class couldn't proceed if the pups refused to participate.

I excitedly proposed this action to the pups in the class. Much to my surprise, most were not only hesitant but unwilling to participate. Fear of consequences outweighed the potential of play time in class. Apparently, I was the only rebel in the pack. Even my popularity, charm and *zooming* amusement weren't enough to gain solidarity with the group. Nevertheless, my inability to assemble my puppy pack wasn't enough to make me give up. I forged onward with my plan for a quiet rebellion even though it meant being on my own in this quest. Belief in the plan for play time gave me the courage and the strength to make it happen. (*I tend to get caught up in the drama.*)

Now, I was never one to really think things out before acting, so this plan never really had success written all over it. Since that possibility hadn't stopped me before, I wasn't going to let it stop me now. So, toward the end of the class, I assumed a defiant, down position on the floor of the facility. The rebellion had begun as soon as my hind quarters hugged the floor as if anchored by sheer will power. One by one, the dogs left the building while sending soulful glances in my direction. Their eyes expressed either admiration or guilt because the rebellion was left up to me to sustain. Any gain on my part would be theirs, yet total punishment would be mine. Not such a bad outcome for an onlooker, but I didn't care. I had an important goal, and that goal was to win play time in Puppy Continuing.

In hindsight, I never once thought about how I would convey my demands to the instructor, the assistants and B.C. All they saw was a defiant pup who was refusing to leave the building. What was I thinking? Apparently, little or no thought went into this endeavor. Once my hind quarters hit the floor, I wasn't able to extricate myself from the situation with any sense of pride. So, I just did nothing but hug the floor while various methods to move me were attempted. Happy voices with encouraging words and the nearby scent of dried liver filled my nostrils as the adults tried to lure me from my silent protest. Since positive reinforcement was the key element in this training facility, I knew that I was safe from being physically dragged from my position on the floor.

Nevertheless, what happened next was completely unexpected and caught me totally off guard. When happy voices and gourmet treats didn't work, the humans decided to leave the building without me. One by one, they headed

I'm in big trouble now.

toward the back door of the facility. While I hugged the floor at the other end of the room, they decided to shut off the lights one section at a time. Apparently, there is no fair play in quiet protests, and I never saw that tactic coming. As the lights were gradually turned off, I was left in the dark by well-trained challengers. I could tell that this was not the first time a pup led such a singular revolt. Not only were the humans prepared for my quiet rebellion, they were also experts in this form of puppy warfare.

Needless to say, as the room got darker and darker, I gave up my floor position even though my demand for play time wasn't met. In fact, it wasn't even heard by my challengers. Acknowledging my defeat, I surrendered and slowly walked to the back door while dragging my leash behind me. I couldn't believe that they were actually going to leave me all by myself in that room because of my defiance. When I turned the corner and reached the back door, B.C. was there waiting for me along with the instructor. I felt a lot better knowing that they really weren't going to leave me alone in the dark. However, as we silently made our way to the car, disappointment filled the air.

Fortunately, all was not lost. I didn't win this battle for play time, but I did gain some insight into human behavior. I

I learned a valuable lesson.

learned that I could control them to some extent with refusals, and that was an extremely valuable piece of information for the future. What I had to work on was better planning for getting what I wanted as well as a way to communicate my demands when in the midst of any future rebellious endeavors. Now, I had the art of refusing as a special tool for attempting to get my way, and all I had to do was to perfect it and use it wisely. (*That sounded a bit bratty…even for me!*) While I lost this silent protest for play time, I gained helpful insights into strategies, and that was something more valuable than play time.

The ride home was filled with unrelenting silence as I sulked in my crate at the back of the car. If I had planned my quiet rebellion before putting it into action, I might have been somewhat successful. However, all was not lost. I wasn't expelled from the training class, still planned *zooming* antics to amuse the class and could hold my head high the next time I saw my classmates. I, alone, attempted to gain something that would benefit all of us, but that just didn't happen. In one sense, it wasn't a failed endeavor because failure was the result of not trying at all. I definitely tried my best, but this time, it just wasn't good enough for success. My next venture, however, will be very well-planned. That much I can guarantee…

Next time I'll know what to do.

10

Kennel Korner

While my short-lived rebellion for play time in the Puppy Continuing class caused a bit of a setback in terms of the folks liking me, all was not a total loss. I was still a resident of the sorority house, and no verbal threats were made regarding mailing me back to my original kennel home. In spite of consequences in the form of time-outs, my life remained pretty much the same.

I attempted to gain some headway in terms of "Operation Like Me" in the weeks that followed by limiting my outbursts to the kitchen area. Getting the *zooms* while in the house was a pretty common occurrence for me. Out of respect to the members of the household, I limited my antics to one area since crashing through the entire house and bouncing off walls just wasn't at all appreciated. So far, my only consequence for repeated *zooming* was a time out in my kennel which I really didn't mind because I secretly enjoyed the solitude. Most times, I'd just go directly into my kennel following my kitchen escapades before B.C. could take me there. I don't think she enjoyed my thinking ahead like that since it didn't seem much like a consequence when I put myself in there without any guidance from her. Apparently, I had developed some mind games of my own in the past few weeks, and my tool box of tricks and techniques was getting larger.

Kessen and Brightie had become more accepting of me as time went by. Because of the heavy snowfall, the yard was totally off limits. The cozy kitchen area became our daily

We're learning to get along.

playground for short periods of time while the basement allowed for much longer, chaotic bonding. When the air snapping and jaw sparring got too intense, play was ended before it got out of control. We'd rest a few minutes and then play a little bit more. Kessen often went off to the side and watched Brightie and me flail around since he didn't seem to enjoy the raucous interactions.

Brightie, on the other paw, fully enjoyed the frenzied activity. She offered a play bow in a most impish manner, spun around three times and barked once as her invitation was accepted by me. B.C. did not favor her play bow strategies for fear that I might mimic them, but she really had nothing to worry about. While I considered Brightie's spinning around and barking amusing, it was a waste of energy. However, I accepted her challenge and played until near exhaustion. When I reached that point, I ran and hid behind Kessen. I only did that to make Brightie feel like she was still second in command of the pack, and I surely didn't want to hurt her feelings by besting her in a skirmish. She was my soul mate, friend and confidant, and nothing was going to spoil that relationship.

Due to my reckless behavior, I spent a great deal of time in my kennel for time outs. Because of my incarceration, Kessen and Brightie began positioning themselves on either side of my kennel to share stories. We jokingly called it Kennel Korner since I was in the kennel, and the kennel was in the corner. It wasn't the most creative title for our special place and time, but it served its purpose. I really wanted to talk about my dreams for athletic achievement with them but had to be cautious about my sharing at such an early stage of our friendship. They were just beginning to fully accept me as part of the household, and I didn't want to jeopardize that. As a result, they did most of the sharing which surprisingly proved to be great entertainment during my kennel confinement.

Kessen talked about all of the dogs who visited the house in the past, and how each brought a different level of excitement and enjoyment to daily life. His eyes actually sparkled with excitement as he recounted fond memories of those events. Surprisingly, Kessen was quite outspoken about his arrival from California in the middle of the Midwest winter. Coming from such a warm climate, his introduction to snow, wind and ice was most shocking to his system. However, he adapted quickly and found a loving home here in the sorority house even though it wasn't named that as yet. As a potential assistance dog in training, he had many adventures in various public places that included restaurants, movie theaters, malls, libraries and many office buildings. He even went on a two week, cross country trip to California and back. What an awesome experience that must have been!

Participation with his mom and dad in numerous high school demonstrations highlighting the work of an assistance dog was of utmost importance to Kessen. He loved the attention of the students and always put his best paw forward when given commands. He had countless adventures while being in the public eye as a potential

Kessen loved sharing his stories.

assistance dog and would share many of them with me in the months to come during Kennel Korner.

Following his stay with the folks, Kessen went on to Advanced Training or Puppy College as it was called. Unfortunately while in training, he suffered from severe kennel stress which eventually led to his release from the assistance program. Kessen was just too sensitive for the rigors of the kennel environment in Advanced Training and was devastated by his release. Upon receiving the news of his discharge, Kessen's folks rushed to the facility, immediately adopted him and nursed him back to health. Once he was well again, he was re-trained as a therapy dog and fulfilled his dream of service to others. It might not have been his first dream, but it was still a dream of service come true for him. Helping others was all that mattered.

Turin, another visitor to the household, was a regal, blonde Labrador Retriever who crossed the threshold with spunk and high energy. He was a potential assistance dog in training who loved to run, take long walks twice a day and go to obedience classes without play time. Turin also had the distinction of being the first

Turin was as agile as a circus performer.

canine to jump over the back of the couch in one, swift leap. That incredibly difficult maneuver made him a legend. To this day, that act has never been duplicated by any canine who ever entered the sorority house. After his year of training and socialization came to a close, Turin went on to Puppy College where he eventually was selected for a helping career.

Kessen truly loved a success story especially if it involved service, and knowing this fact made me even more reluctant to tell of my dreams since they didn't involve any form of assistance to others. I'd have to find just the right time to spring that information on my two newest, canine pals.

A few days later while listening to stories at Kennel Korner, I wasn't at all surprised to learn that Brightie's spirited arrival as the first, female pup led not only to the naming of the sorority house, but to her title of Resident Diva as well. Weighing in at only ten pounds, Brightie slept on her back in her kennel. Kessen thought her chubby pink belly looked like a little pork roast. She had the face of an angel

Who could resist that face?

but the lungs of some enormous, feral beast. Her howling lasted for weeks while she expected everyone to do her bidding. Kessen also admitted in a moment of nostalgia that he was a bit smitten by her beauty, her blonde silken coat and dark chocolate brown eyes. He even imagined that perhaps one day when she was older that they might have some romantic connection. That dream, however, was smashed to smithereens very quickly when he was told that she was going to be his adopted sister. That romantic possibility never crossed his mind again. Yet another dream of Kessen's was dashed with the strength of one word... sister! Instead, he willingly assumed the role of older brother and protector of this tiny imp. He sure knew how to adjust!

Kessen also shared that when Brightie first came to the house, she was a bit of a bully and was difficult to train. The folks found out that while she was the first born, she was the smallest in her litter and was picked on by her siblings. In the fight or flight scenario, Brightie chose to fight. As a result, she had great trust issues when she arrived. Surrounded by the love of her human family and Kessen's need to protect her as her big brother, she eventually learned to trust others. In addition to that, both she and Kessen had the help of a special dog named Linus who taught them what only dogs can teach other dogs well...puppy etiquette.

Linus was a stately Golden Retriever who specialized in teaching puppy etiquette to other dogs. (*Now that sounded amazing!*) He spent a full week with both Kessen and Brightie teaching them appropriate behavior. His secret to success was called the Three Step Action Plan. When first encountering a disrespectful pup, he'd make his lips quiver in a bit of a threatening manner. If that wasn't enough to change the

Linus was an incredible dog.

pup's impolite behavior, Linus added a low, menacing growl to the process. Sometimes, those two steps weren't enough to stop the rudeness, so Linus followed the first two steps with a muffled snap…never connecting, but making a definite point. According to Kessen, it worked every time for him but took a little longer with Brightie. On the other paw, Brightie said that it was the other way around in terms of learning from Linus. Despite the fact that they each had their own version of the story, I still found it hilarious.

While Kessen first thought Linus to be the most pompous dog he had ever met, he learned to respect Linus not only for what he knew but for what he was willing to share with other pups. Kessen even tried to mimic Linus' Three Step Action Plan with some of the pups who came to the house, but was unsuccessful due to his inability to make his lips quiver without breaking into fits of laughter or sneezing. Consequently, it wasn't as effective as Linus' approach and only resulted in unrestrained laughter from the pups. Even though Kessen abandoned that technique, he still learned a lot from Linus as did Brightie, but it sure sounded like Kessen learned the most. After all, he did become the leader of the pack.

Hearing all of these wonderful things about Linus, I had hoped that I might meet him one day, but Kessen sadly mentioned that Linus had crossed over the Rainbow Bridge a few years ago. While he was no longer with us, his memory lived on in the hearts of all the dogs who encountered him as well as in his legacy of fostering proper etiquette in pups. According to Kessen, losing Linus was a loss for all canines…especially for those who never got to meet him.

During another Kennel Korner get-together, Brightie talked about another female pup that came to live with them while in training for a career in assistance. Her name was Marnie, and there was a special gentleness about that pup from the minute she crossed the threshold. The ears that framed her pitch-black eyes were the texture of crushed velvet set against the glossy, ebony coat that covered her sleek figure. While that darkened look might seem intimidating to other canines, all Marnie had to do was tilt her head a certain way, and the softness of her face emerged...confirming her gentle and charismatic nature.

According to Brightie, Marnie loved both canines and humans alike. She'd play gently with humans, yet didn't shy away from any lively skirmish in the yard with Kessen and Brightie. She even repeatedly dared to touch Kessen's ring toy and especially enjoyed Kessen's swift reaction to her recurring annoyance. She knew just how far and how fast to run to avoid any punishment for the attention to his ring toy but so enjoyed his reactions to her most playful antics. In spite of her foolishness, both Kessen and Brightie loved Marnie a lot and credited her with the

Marnie was so special.

founding of the annual Tradition of Turmoil during the Christmas holidays.

By all accounts, attempts were made at holiday time to get a picture of all of the dogs together for the annual Christmas card. The camera was ready as were the pups who were wearing special holiday collars with bells jingling from them. Tasty treats were on hand for attention-getting as the pups were positioned in front of the Christmas tree. The fun began when Kessen, Brightie and Marnie were in position, all in the camera's focus and ready for the Christmas card shot. Marnie, who was always the goody-four-paws in the group, would unexpectedly jump on Brightie, and Brightie, in turn, would jump on Kessen. Chaos ensued as all three dogs then ran around the room chasing after each other at full speed. What fun they had until the folks stopped them in their tracks. When calm was once again restored, the dogs were repositioned and another picture was attempted. Just as the click of the camera was about to be heard, Marnie once again rolled over on Brightie, and Brightie, in turn, jumped on Kessen. The race was on again.

Finally, the folks ended the nonsense with stern looks and hands on hips…which means business in the canine world. Rather than have a repeat of the chaos, they positioned Marnie on the other side of Kessen. This eliminated the possibility of another frolic with Brightie, and the problem was solved for that year. However, Kessen and Brightie so enjoyed the activity that they decided to do it every year in memory of Marnie. The Tradition of Turmoil lives on with the annual Christmas photo.

The Tradition of Turmoil lives on.

Marnie left them a few months later for Puppy College. While they never saw her again, they heard that she, too, became an assistance dog for someone in need. Both Kessen and Brightie had great pride in her achievement. Once again, I saw the delight not only in Kessen's eyes but in Brightie's as well. There was something very strange about this fascination with assistance that permeated the thoughts and actions of all who lived under this roof.

Kennel Korner chatter was such a valuable source of information in the weeks that followed. I found out that many dogs crossed the threshold of the sorority house throughout the years either for a weekend visit, a few weeks or for many months. Most went on to some form of service for others, and what eventually evolved between Kessen and Brightie was the Socialization Squad. Coming together as a team, they would carry on Linus' work and help socialize the pups that came to stay with them. While they could never adequately take Linus' place with regard to teaching puppy etiquette, they would do their best to help the pups in residence. They complemented each other in terms of temperament since Kessen was the stern disciplinarian while Brightie provided the comic relief. Each had a special way of connecting with the pups, and they took great pride in their positions as co-captains of the squad. The Socialization Squad was their special form of service to others, and they were definitely good at it. After all, they kept my attention, and that wasn't an easy task.

They really work together as a team.

These bits of information about the dogs just heightened my curiosity regarding their need to help others.

Why didn't I have that desire? Were my dreams of athletic achievement, trophies and awards clouding what was important in my life? Kennel Korner conversations brought up quite a few questions about my career path as well as the beginnings of some nagging doubts regarding my future plans.

Kessen and Brightie really presented a lot of information regarding past visitors, and in doing that, shared even more about themselves. I believed that I reached an entirely new level of understanding of both of them and especially felt that a degree of trust now existed among us. Perhaps it was now my turn to share my dreams even though they didn't include service to others. Would Kessen and Brightie accept my dreams as being worthwhile endeavors because they were mine to achieve? Might they consider my dreams to be foolish attempts for shallow rewards, and would telling them change our newly-formed relationships? These were very serious questions. Nevertheless, if I were to ever get a chance to fulfill my dreams, I'd need their help. First and foremost, I'd need their acceptance of my dreams in order to move forward towards my career choice. Sharing my dreams with them was definitely a risk, but I just had to take that chance...

11

Name Game

The weeks passed, the snow was melted and the sun actually shined for a few moments throughout the day. The dismal days of winter seemed to be nearing the end of what I believed was quite a long, blustery season. So many things had happened during the past winter...events that would undoubtedly change my life forever.

While I spent a great deal of time in my kennel every day due to my overly enthusiastic behavior, I still hadn't told Kessen and Brightie about my dreams for athletic achievement. Giving hints as to my skills in the form of my jumping, running and twirling while in the house and yard made no reasonable impact on them. In fact, the opposite occurred. Kessen believed my noncompliance in the house was an intentional symptom of lack of discipline. Brightie, on the other paw, thought that I was perhaps a bit slower in the brain department and just didn't catch on to rules and regulations as readily as other pups who stayed in the house. Nevertheless, neither assessment was complimentary and, in some respects, was downright insulting. Just because they weren't picking up on my obvious cues didn't make me rebellious or not the brightest bulb in the lamp. I originally believed that communicating with them was the easy part, but that certainly wasn't turning out to be the case. Consequently, if I couldn't make them recognize my goals, how would I ever make B.C. and G.C. understand? My lack of communication skills was a major detriment to sharing my dreams.

Somehow, I'd make them all understand, and sharing my dreams with Kessen and Brightie was an essential element to the success of my plan. While I knew that Kennel Korner time was the best opportunity to share my dreams, it posed the greatest risk to our newly acquired friendship. Since Kessen and Brightie had so many interesting stories to share, I would just have to wait for the right moment to spring it on them

A few days later in one of our Kennel Korner chitchats, Kessen spoke about the Name Game. Based upon a dog's predominant behaviors, appearances, silly antics or tendencies, the folks selected nicknames for each of the dogs. For example, Kessen was given the nickname of Box Boy when he was very young because he loved to either stand or lay on a plastic box while

He's called the Box Boy.

he played. As he grew older, the name changed to Special K-Man since he was not only a conscientious pup but the designated leader of the pack.

He's the T-Man.

When Turin was in the house, he was called T-Man because of his attempts to defy gravity with his airborne leaps and daily, mischievous behavior. Marnie, the sweet black Lab was called Marnie Google. That was a strange choice, but it had something to do with her beautiful eyes or what the folks termed her "goo-goo-googliest eyes." Once again, I don't get it, but I don't speak Human and probably never will.

She's our Marnie Google.

Brightie was called Brightie Girl because she used her femininity by fluttering her long eyelashes to get Kessen to do her bidding whenever she pleased. Brightie was definitely my kind of special gal. While that feminine route wasn't my usual style, I admired her ability to get what she wanted by using her feminine charm. I, on the other paw, relied completely

I have my feminine, winning ways.

127

upon my athletic prowess. Unfortunately, that talent was only getting me more kennel time. Perhaps my enthusiastic approach to getting my way needed some modifications.

Now, I was curious as to what B.C. and G.C. considered as a nickname for me. Kessen and Brightie looked as if they knew something but didn't want to tell me. I insisted that they share what special nickname or nicknames for me were being bantered about the household. For the first time since I arrived, Kessen actually looked very apologetic and really didn't want to tell me. Nevertheless, I insisted that he share his information since I expected something really unique that reflected my skill set. After all, I demonstrated my athletic talents on a daily basis. Kessen's reluctance was likely due to the fact that he was envious of the possibilities, and I was positive that my nickname was both exceptional and descriptive of my extraordinary talents.

To my great surprise, my thinking was totally off the puppy path again. That information really concerned me on a number of significant levels. Was I losing my perspective as well as my ability to make good judgments? That couldn't possibly be happening to me all because of silly nicknames. This never happened to me when I was in the kennel with Calm and Calmer. Living with humans is not only exhausting but apparently mind-bending as well.

Kessen finally relented and shared the nicknames being tossed around the household. Brightie braced herself behind Kessen in case there was any blow back from the forthcoming information. Based on my behaviors, the names ranged from The Black Tornado, Dust Demon, Izz-Max to the most insulting...the Izz-Manian Devil. How could these people be so far off the puppy path in their assessment of me? My actions demonstrated athletic dexterity that related to exceptional nicknames not such derogatory possibilities. Spinning, jumping, leaping, twirling and running at top speeds were powerful attributes and not something to be disrespected. Granted, doing these things in the house on a daily basis wasn't the most productive way to win friends, but I deserved a break in the Name Game...not insults. After all, I was a champion athlete in the making and worked on my skills to attain perfection. Just because I wasn't able to communicate my goals to the household members wasn't any reason to give me such un-inspired labels.

To say I was disappointed was an understatement of huge proportions. What did it take to make B.C. and G.C. understand that my actions were skillful and not disruptive in nature? Not only was I disappointed but also very upset. Those nicknames were hurtful, but I wasn't going to let Kessen and Brightie see my sensitive side. (*I didn't even know I had one until now.*) Up to this point, I had been a rough and tumbling, energetic tom-girl bent upon future, athletic accomplishments. Never would I let them see my sadness nor my newly discovered vulnerability. Consequently, I just pretended that the nicknames didn't matter to me at all. I would be a champion in spite of those names. When I started winning trophies and ribbons, they'd see how wrong they were.

Kessen and Brightie had such looks of sadness after sharing those nicknames with me, but I assured them that it didn't matter to me. My name was Izzy, and I didn't need something as silly and foolish as a nickname to make me feel important. That being said, I pretended to curl up for a morning nap, and they slowly walked away to their own places in the house.

As if on cue, B.C. entered my kitchen area, released me from my kennel and allowed me some yard time. How did she know that I needed to be alone with my sadness? It was strange that the initial, fluttering *tingle* that I felt when she spent time with me was getting stronger each day. It wasn't the same as with my birth mother, but it was similar. Truth be told, I really liked B.C. in spite of her mind games and unsuitable nicknames. Perhaps I'd have to find an appropriate nick name for her. After all, I could play the Name Game as well as anyone else.

So with my head down and tail tucked, I went out into the yard and found refuge in the Red Twig Dogwoods that were now sprouting leaves and forming a barrier between the fence rails and the huge yard. The twigs offered some bit of shelter but were still hazardous in terms of their potential for poking out my eyes. Nevertheless, it was the perfect spot for my pity party, and I was both the party girl and only guest.

Suddenly, I heard a voice from the other side of the fence, and to my surprise, it was Sammy...the neighborhood sage. As he ambled closer to the fence rails, I hoped that he was joining my pity party to offer solace in my moment of gloom. Sammy was truly wise and would certainly share my disappointment or so I thought. Once again, I was way off that puppy path with my assessment of his reason to visit.

I welcomed him to my pity party and shared my thoughts about the nicknames chosen by B.C. and G.C. I just knew that he'd understand and might even sympathize with me. Apparently, Sammy had other thoughts on the matter. According to him, if nicknames were given on the basis of behavior and I continued to run at top speeds, spin, twirl and jump while in the house, then the nicknames were both descriptive and fairly accurate. He felt that nicknames were never meant to be hurtful but jovial signs of camaraderie among friends. The ones they considered for me just happen to brush my coat the wrong way since I didn't think they were funny at all.

Sammy felt that B.C. and G.C. played the Name Game fair and square based on my household behavior. In addition to that, he felt that I was the insensitive one having given unflattering nicknames to them...beginning with Bad Cop and Good Cop and ending with B.C. and G.C. To my surprise, I had played the Name Game and didn't even realize it. Actually looking at it through Sammy's eyes was a bit of an awakening for me. Was I actually feeling a tinge

It's just my opinion.

of guilt at this point for the nicknames I had given them? I was not ready to visit the Doghouse of Guilt (D.O.G.) since I was still adjusting to the possibility of having a sensitive side to my personality. Too many new and mixed feelings were circling my mind, and Sammy's pity party evaluation was not what I hoped to get from him.

In my defense, even though I had been an unknowing participant in the Name Game, I still didn't think I deserved the nicknames being tossed around the house. As much as I didn't want to admit to being wrong, Sammy was definitely correct in that my names for the humans were not very kind…descriptive perhaps, but not particularly nice. Obviously, I did to them what they did to me, and I never realized it until now. In spite of my raucous behavior and somewhat self-centered thinking, I still maintained a rather vague sense of justice and fairness. I had to figure out a way to make it right, but where to begin? Perhaps Sammy, in

I'll need help with this problem.

his infinite wisdom, might offer some suggestions for accomplishing this.

I was finally right about something since Sammy had some brilliant thoughts on that issue as well. He lapsed into a story about Kessen, who as a puppy, had a similar dilemma in the name department for the people who took him into their home. He felt disloyal to his birth mother if he referred to his new family members as mom and dad but didn't know what else to call them. Apparently as a pup, Kessen was just as confused as I was, and the thought of Kessen being confused was a tough bone to chew. However, he was a puppy at the time, and puppies did foolish things. My actions on a daily basis definitely confirmed that premise.

Sammy focused his penetrating eyes on me and said. "Listen Izzy...and listen well because I'll only say this once. Have these people cared for you, kept you safe and warm, fed you regularly and, above all, given you unconditional love in spite of your reckless and wild behavior? If you answer *yes* to all of those, then you have to acknowledge that they consider you a part of their family. Because of this commitment to you, they deserve names other than B.C. and G.C., and calling them mom and dad isn't being disloyal to your birth mother. They just took over where your birth mother left off and showed you the love that she wasn't able to give you after you were taken from her. The sooner you accepted that, the happier you will be. It worked for Kessen, and it will surely work for you."

I listened attentively to Sammy and tried to process everything he asked of me. Ultimately, he was right, and as much as I hated to admit it, I was wrong not to choose better names for them considering what they did for me on a daily basis. They carried on with my care since my birth mother wasn't able to do it. I never knew my father, and my mother was all I had when I was younger. In many ways, I wasn't ready to let go of that strong *tingle* signifying my birth mother's love. That feeling seemed to keep me safe and warm when I felt alone or sad. Following Sammy's logic, I really didn't have to let that feeling go. Perhaps I just had to make room in my heart for another form of *tingle*...like the one I felt the day of my arrival when B.C. covered my kennel so I might privately grieve for the loss of my family. That little flutter of a *tingle* should have been my biggest clue for an appropriate name for her. Why didn't I recognize it at the time? Perhaps Brightie was right in her assessment of me in that I was quite possibly not the brightest bulb in the lamp. All of this thinking was exhausting and not at all what I expected of a pity party.

While Sammy didn't wait for my answer to his questions, he knew the truth would help me through this nickname nonsense. His wisdom was such a help to me at a time when my emotions governed my actions. My pity party was over, and as far as I was concerned, B.C. and G.C. would now be known as Mom and Dad to me. I'd have to get used to calling them that, but I always accomplish what I set out to do.

Their mind games most likely weren't going to stop, and my potential nicknames wouldn't necessarily change because my behavior wasn't going to change...not yet anyway. I had to continue my quest for athletic perfection in spite of some silly nicknames, but I would certainly change my names for them out of respect for everything they did for me. That was definitely the right thing to do. Since they would continue what they were doing, and my behavior wasn't going to change, I considered that a draw in terms of the Name Game tallies...

It's the right thing to do.

12

Wait For The Moment

My public outings had begun. Long walks to the park, visits to restaurants, trips to the library, weekly attendance at church services and numerous other places filled my days. I didn't know why I had to wear that cape, but Brightie informed me that it signified my potential as a future assistance dog, and wearing it allowed me to visit public places. The fact that the cape pertained to a future in assistance didn't change my mind about my athletic possibilities. However, hearing that the cape wasn't a sign of some abnormality was a great relief since Brightie's harsh assessment about the possibility of my not being the brightest bulb in the lamp frequently preyed on my mind. Because I just didn't take rules seriously, I still had numerous time outs in the kennel due to my continued *zooming* in the house. In my defense, this body was a finely tuned instrument of athletic potential that had to be nurtured on a daily basis. (*Who believed stuff like that? It was a stretch even for me!*)

I just had to tell Kessen and Brightie about my athletic dreams, but I had to wait for the right moment, and that moment had to be soon. They really needed to know that what they considered extreme and reckless behavior on my part wasn't reckless at all. Although I ran around the house at

137

great speeds whenever I could, my actions had meaning and

direction in terms of my future. I wasn't just an ill-disciplined, boisterous pup taking advantage of a nice household and causing chaos on a daily basis; I was an athlete in training.

They really need to understand.

The moment of truth came unexpectedly after a surprising, book-selling gig at a dog festival. The event was held in a nearby park, and my newly dubbed mom and dad were selling the book that my mom had written about Kessen. The sun shined brightly on the multi-colored, pop-up tents that surrounded a huge, grassy demonstration area. Barking and howling dogs of all sizes and breeds were everywhere in this huge, outdoor playground. Some ran ahead of their owners extending to the full length of their leashes while taking in the sights and sounds, and others remained tangled in their retractable leashes unable to enjoy the freedom of a loose leash. I also saw quite a few dogs walking obediently at the side of their owners. That compliant style of walking reminded me of my typical mode of walking when out in public and wearing my cape. Not a lot of opportunity for extreme fun in that walking position, but it was better than nothing.

There was so much going on around, behind and in front of me that I darted back and forth in the booth so as not to miss anything. Seeing how enthusiastic I was about the festivities, my mom decided to take me for a walk around the grounds. I didn't even care that I had to walk nicely on the leash. All that mattered was that I was going to see everything that this wonderland of dog fun had to offer.

Booths of all sizes and shapes filled the area offering magnificent treasures that pertained to dogs and the dog world. There were brightly decorated treats, bones of all sizes and shapes, ornamental collars, colorful leashes, car harnesses, multiple samples of food, dog beds, training opportunities and even dog's clothing with sports logos. Naming all of the different items wasn't possible because there were so many. There were also puppy adoption opportunities where optimistic pups strained at their fencing giving each passerby loving looks and hopeful glances. Others just slept in their enclosures giving the onlooker the sense of a calm and respectful demeanor amidst the chaos. (*Those pups were probably just tired.*)

All in all, it was an incredible sight, and the aromas of freshly popped corn filled the air and drove my taste buds wild as we traveled around the festival. It was an event of grand proportions, but what I didn't realize was that my focus on athletic potential was a lot closer than expected.

As we turned a corner, there was an announcement regarding a disc dog demonstration in the center arena. Did I hear correctly? A disc dog demonstration? That was right up my doghouse of future plans. I, too, wanted to fly through the air, twist and reach for a thrown, circular object to reveal my expertise in that area. This happening was monumental, and it was clearly destiny that brought me here at this specific moment...or was it something else?

While my mom played numerous mind games on a daily basis, maybe her ability to read minds was an element that I didn't know existed before today. If that were true, then perhaps she already knew of my dreams for athletic achievement, and this dog festival was just a way of communicating her awareness of my dreams to me. It was a distinct possibility, and that thought made this day even better in terms of my future.

We positioned ourselves along the fence line where the demonstration was to take place, and I had a clear view of the arena. A man, standing in the middle of the field, held a number of rubber-like discs, and at his side was a trim, beautifully marked, black and white Border Collie. When the handler gave the signal to the Border Collie, the dog went out into the middle of the arena, turned to face him and waited for direction. While waiting, the dog crouched to the ground with his hind quarters slightly elevated and his eyes locked like a laser beam on the disc. Not wanting to forget anything, I attempted to imitate the dog's stance and hugged the ground in a similar, crouching position. As soon as the handler flung the disc, the dog's eyes locked onto the target like a heat-seeking missile. He sprinted forward, leapt an incredible height into the air, twirled around and caught the flying object in his mouth. In my total excitement, I lunged forward as if jumping for a disc only to be stopped suddenly by the fence. Bouncing backwards brought me back to reality, but I had successfully duplicated both the dog's crouching position and the lunge into the air. Unfortunately, that fence barrier thwarted my lunge, but I definitely will remember all of the details. My mom just gave me a puzzled look after I bounced off the fence, but in truth, she was used to my doing strange things.

That amazing Border Collie then returned for another enthusiastic pass at the thrown disc. This time, he jumped even higher, twirled even faster, caught the disc and ran back to his handler...only to climb up the handler's back and do an astounding balancing feat on the handler's shoulders! The applause was deafening, and I imagined myself sitting on a handler's shoulders taking in the ovation after my own display of athletic prowess. The experience was exhilarating, and I had to force myself back into a good walking position when the demonstration ended. I didn't care because I saw my future in that exhibition, and I couldn't wait to tell Kessen and Brightie about the entire experience.

We then followed the crowd to the other end of the field where we saw this huge pool of water with an adjacent dock. It was the largest pool I had ever seen, and the overall size was a bit intimidating. My experience with pools was limited to a few bath tub dips and a few jumps into the baby pool in the yard. The enormous size of this one made my mouth go dry. I saw various dogs lined up on the dock and realized that yet another of my dreams was coming true. These were dock diving dogs, and I was going to see them in action for the very first time. I had heard about these dogs while in the kennel with Calm and Calmer but had never seen them actually diving into the water.

My excitement grew as I had a great view of the entire dock and pool. The first contestant, a black Labrador Retriever, approached the starting position. There were very strict rules about behavior and impulse control in this contest. Even though the Lab was anxious to go for his first dive, he remained in an excited sitting position on a short leash at his handler's side. At that point, the dog was taken to the location of the exit ramp in the pool so as not to be confused where to exit following his jump into the water. The Lab was then returned to the starting line on the dock and placed in a controlled sitting position. Tension filled the air as the handler, holding a toy, unleashed the dog and walked to the edge of the dock facing the pool. The dog's eyes were locked on his handler in anticipation of his signal to begin the jump. I was so excited that my hackles didn't know what to do as they were dancing up and down my back from tip to tail. I think my paws were even sweating from the excitement. (*They did that a lot lately.*) For once, I was glad that I was on a short leash because there was no fence to stop me if I decided to take the plunge along with the Lab.

Once ready, the handler flung the toy as far as he could into the pool and gave the release command. The Lab ran to the edge of the dock and leapt as far as he could across the length of the pool area. It was a phenomenal leap across the water both in terms of speed and distance. The dog splashed happily into the water, retrieved the toy and made his way to the exit ramp. It was an incredible leap and might not be beaten by any other contestants. What an exhibition of strength, skill and bravado. I had never seen a dog jump that far or into such an enormous pool of water. Other dogs followed and jumped great distances as well, but none challenged the distance of the first Lab. Clearly, he was the winner of this demonstration. I thought my leaps and jumps were great when I was in the kennel with my siblings, but nothing I ever did compared to these dock diving athletes.

I was bewildered by this exhibition since my jumps in the kennel area and yard paled in comparison to the jumps I saw today. In light of that realization, did I even like water enough to dive into such a great expanse of it? As I recalled, my last bath wasn't all that enjoyable...mostly due to the water. Dunking for rubber balls in the baby pool in the yard wasn't particularly pleasant either. It was frustrating because the rubber balls got so slippery in the water that I wasn't able to grab them without gulping large amounts of water. If I did manage to grab one, the bouts of coughing that followed the gulping of water caused me to drop the ball into the water again. How was I supposed to dive for some object in a gigantic, deep pool of water if I couldn't even successfully grab a slippery ball in a baby pool?

Perhaps dock diving just wasn't in my future, and it was better to eliminate it now and concentrate on other areas. Narrowing my choices would only make me stronger in whatever area was best for me. Seeing this dock diving demonstration was so helpful in terms of realistically looking at athletic endeavors. I was lucky to have actually seen it in order to acknowledge that it just wasn't the career choice for me.

So, dock diving was definitely out of the career plan, and my focus was now on being a disc dog or perhaps an agility dog. Surprisingly, my decision to eliminate dock diving didn't sadden me. After seeing the size of that pool, I really didn't want to dive into that huge amount of water. After this water-world exhibition, I had new found respect for my water bowls at home...those I handled with ease.

Just when I didn't think this day could get any better, another announcement was made about an additional demonstration in the center arena that was surrounded by the fence...that same fence that blocked my attempt at the disc dog demonstration. The arena now contained an obstacle course that consisted of open and closed tunnels, hurdles of various heights, a regulation seesaw, an elevated dog walk, weave poles, a tire jump, a few other forms of equipment and finally ending with something called a pause table.

Yikes!!

Once again, my dreams were coming true...it was a special agility demonstration. At this point, I was so over stimulated that my eyes were rolling around in their sockets, and I don't believe that I was ever this excited in my life. My mom was either playing a truly evil mind game on me by bringing me to this dog festival while wearing my assistance cape or showing me the proverbial light at the end of the agility tunnel of my dreams. At this moment in time, it didn't matter what her motives were because today, she was tops in my treat bowl.

Once again, we positioned ourselves along the fence line. This time, I recognized my limitations in terms of breaching the fence. Time stood still for me as I waited with great anticipation since this demonstration might give me a glance into my future. The first dog, a smooth coated, black and white Fox Terrier and his handler entered the arena. When the signal was given, the exhibition began. Both speed and efficient maneuvering of the equipment determined the winner, so precise following of the handler's direction was required. The Fox Terrier followed the handler's direction over the first hurdle as if on wings, went through the open tunnel, advanced to the elevated dog walk, flew across another hurdle, sped through the closed tunnel, soared through the tire jump, scrambled up and down the seesaw and finished with a perfect sitting position on the pause table.

My mouth was actually dry from the excitement of the performance as both the dog and handler enjoyed the applause that followed. I was in awe of the incredible talent and strength it took to perform that way in front of all of these spectators. The next two dogs, an amazing Springer Spaniel and an energetic Miniature Schnauzer, won the approval of the audience as well. It was apparent that dogs of all sizes and shapes participated in this type of activity. All of the dogs were just wonderful, and I wanted to be just like them...fast, precise and obedient. I believed that I could be fast and precise without too much trouble, but I really had to work on the concept of being obedient. Since I wasn't given those silly nicknames because I was an example of canine compliance, the notion of being obedient was a bit of a stretch for me.

However, I was a determined canine and would do whatever I had to do in order to be a champion athlete. After reliving the events of the day in my mind, perhaps working the disc dog angle was more my style since jumping, twirling and spinning were my specialties. In any event, I couldn't

I'm ready to do this.

wait to meet with Kessen and Brightie to tell them about the various events as well as discuss my future plans as an athlete rather than an assistance dog. I no longer had to wait for the right moment to share my dreams since this dog festival gave me the perfect opportunity in more ways than one. Going to this dog festival and seeing these different events was a definite sign from the canine gods that I was to move forward with my career decisions.

Sharing my dreams with Kessen and Brightie was extremely important since I needed their understanding, support and help in order to be successful. Their friendship meant a lot to me, and choosing a career dealing with athletic endeavors instead of assistance to others would definitely be a great disappointment to them. However, I'd have to take that risk and truly hoped that after seeing how hard I worked toward reaching my goals, their disappointment would someday change to acceptance and possibly admiration. Given time and understanding, I just knew that day would come...

13

Give a Little

I was exhausted following the thrilling day at the dog festival. So much excitement and fun crammed into one day was a bit overwhelming...even for me. While I was eager to tell Kessen and Brightie about my day, I dreaded the possibility of fallout from sharing my dreams with them. However, it was clear that I had to have that conversation as soon as possible. Unfortunately, I seemed to have more courage while at the festival than I did now. Perhaps after having a good nap, my bravery would re-emerge to the level of facing any consequences from telling my career plans to my new friends.

When the folks and I got home from the festival, Kessen and Brightie were waiting at the front door to hear about my day. I pretended to look extremely exhausted in an effort to avoid talking with them. Although I felt a bit cowardly by doing that, it served a real purpose. They understood how tiring outings were and agreed to meet me later at Kennel Korner. Kessen assumed that I'd run around the house and bounce off a few walls which would inevitably end up with my being put in the kennel. (*That was such a harsh assumption but fairly accurate.*) I definitely surprised him by walking right into my kennel when we got home. In the meantime, I would take a brief nap and rehearse my speech to them which had to be flawless in detail and heartfelt in terms of emotion. Those details were the keys to convincing them that my dreams were really worth their understanding, help and support. I only hoped that I could pull that off given that I had been a bit of a goofball since my arrival at the sorority house. Serious conversations with me were, for the most part, non-existent.

My nap was brief because the inevitable disclosure of my career plans caused my usual, deep sleep to be restless and not at all refreshing. I just wanted to regain some courage and tell them what needed to be said…once and for all. I was never one to be fearful of risks or consequences before coming here, but I never faced something as important as this either.

As I awakened from my nap, Kessen and Brightie were sitting on opposite sides of my kennel and were quite anxious to hear about my escapades at the dog festival. When they were in training for assistance and allowed public access, they had a lot of experiences like mine and missed doing that now. Hearing about my outing was the next best thing to being there, and they were truly interested in what I had to say about my day. Now, I had friends who actually cared about me and my day's events. Since I had been such a loner in the past, their attention was a new and welcomed experience for me.

I tried to describe in as much detail as I could in terms of the grounds, the colorful tents, the items for sale and especially the aromas. My cape still smelled of popcorn and, to be honest, made it a bit more appealing to me. Up until now, I mostly hid when I saw the cape and didn't really enjoy wearing it. Because Kessen was able to go to public places while wearing his cape, he thought it had magical powers. Personally, I didn't feel that way at all about my cape. I believed that the color didn't adequately reflect the intensity of my eyes nor did its boxy shape enhance my svelte figure. In any event, I hoped that the popcorn aroma would remain in my cape for a very long time. That would not only remind me of this special day but would also add a somewhat magical component to the fabric. I certainly wouldn't hide from a cape as awesome as that!

Next, I told them about the spectacular disc dog, dock diving and agility demonstrations. While Kessen wasn't surprised that I bounced off the fence while watching the disc dog exhibition, Brightie was totally amused by it and wished that she could have seen it. Witnessing our mom's expression when that happened, on the other paw, would have been worth a huge, treat bag full of laughs around the food bowls. It was unfortunate that my telling of the events only gave Kessen and Brightie a second paw experience, but they enjoyed hearing about them anyway.

Nevertheless, I told them as much as I could remember and mentioned that I had something very serious to discuss with them…something that not only had to do with my future plans but also with their friendships. Since I rarely looked or sounded serious, I had their immediate attention. Both dogs settled into relaxed positions and were intrigued by what I might tell them.

It was difficult to begin with them staring intently at me, but telling about my early kennel days of high jumping, fast twirling, spinning and lunging was the appropriate way to start. Even as a very young pup in my first kennel home, I knew that my athletic skills were gifts that no other pups in the kennel possessed. Even my brothers and sisters couldn't duplicate any of my high-flying actions. Wasn't that proof enough that athletic achievement was my calling?

Since Kessen's piercing eyes had already glazed over and Brightie was thoroughly confused, I skipped ahead to my moving into the sorority house. I reminded them that I repeatedly caused chaos due to my *zooming* in the house, enjoyed spinning, twirling and jumping my way through the hallways and disregarded

Where is she going with this?

all rules of deportment. Ricocheting off doors was definitely my specialty. Since I never knew when the bedroom doors would be opened or closed, my speed never matched my ability to stop in time. Nevertheless, I wasn't running wild as they thought. I was honing my athletic skills, and the doors just got in my way. (*Lending humor to that bit of information was my dubious attempt to break the tension of the moment.*)

While I thought that a dash of amusement might be the perfect bone-breaker for the telling of my future plans, my judgment was once again flawed. (*That seemed to happen quite often these days.)* Seeing as Brightie always found a little hilarity in most of my frolics, I wasn't really concerned about her reaction. As expected, Kessen found no humor in either the explanation of my past kennel antics or current household behavior. On the other paw, I wasn't going to let his piercing gaze deter me from what I had to tell them. I figured that since these explanations weren't making any sense to them, I'd just tell them my plans and see what happened.

I slowly sat back on my haunches, assumed a confident

There…it's done!

position, slowly took an extremely deep breath that almost turned into a full, reverse sneeze and just told them that I wasn't going to be an assistance dog. My life's calling was to be either a champion disc dog or a competitive agility dog. I had all of the necessary skills and determination for great success in either event but needed fine tuning of my athletic ability, the total support of my friends and help with communicating my plans to our mom and dad. While I believed that a future in assistance was a noble endeavor, it just wasn't for me. I had championship competitions, trophies and awards in my sights, and those were definitely my future goals.

For the very first time since I moved into the sorority house, neither Kessen nor Brightie had anything to say. At the very least, I expected a disapproving lecture, some looks of disappointment or arguments against my future plans. Instead, they just stared intently at me in an attempt to digest my explosive news. After a few moments, Brightie began licking her lip indicating her stress over what I had just shared. With a look of frustration on his face, Kessen just shook his head, turned away and left our Kennel Korner area. Brightie, not knowing what to do or say, followed him out of the room with her head down and tail hanging low. Turning their backs on me and leaving the room were such sad sights for me to behold.

Silence filled the air around my kennel, and I was left alone with my thoughts. Getting the silent treatment from them was totally unexpected. In my mind, we all had to give a little in terms of our plans for the future. Kessen and Brightie had their own opportunities for careers. Even though their vocations were predetermined by their assistance dog organization, they were the right choices for them. Service was surely their calling, but it definitely wasn't mine. Assistance to others required unique qualities in a dog, and I just didn't have them. Both Kessen and Brightie had those special gifts and lived their dreams in terms of helping others. My dreams were very different from theirs and perhaps even looked shallow to them since mine involved winning trophies and ribbons. All the same, I was entitled to my dreams just as much as they were entitled to theirs.

Why was I now feeling guilty about putting personal possessions and laurels over service to others? Living in this sorority house changed me in so many ways and adjusting to those changes wasn't easy. Recently discovering that I had a sensitive side when faced with unkind nicknames was so unlike my nature. Nothing ever bothered me before because I only answered to myself for my actions. Nowadays, I found myself wanting approval from Kessen and Brightie as well as experiencing feelings that I never had before coming here. In addition to that, I felt guilty because they disapproved of my choices.

What was happening to me that I now sought the approval of others? Being needy, caring about others and seeking approval were certainly not aspects of my personality in the past. Was this sorority house experience life-changing rather than just a pathway to my career goals? My life here changed me faster than I imagined. Because of that, my choice was to either accept the changes or take a different path from everything that was safe and familiar to me.

Reacting to Kessen and Brightie's response was the least of my worries since the changes in me affected my future plans. Up until now, those plans were mine and mine alone. Now I had a family and their feelings to consider. Was I expected to give up my dreams to regain harmony in the household or give up my new family in pursuit of my dreams? How could I possibly choose between the two? I had no one to turn to for advice and just didn't know what to do...

14

Feeling Down

Two weeks had passed since my explosive, career news hit the household airwaves. While in the house and yard, Kessen and Brightie remained polite yet somewhat aloof towards me. At times, I thought Brightie wanted to stop and chat with me, but that didn't happen. She politely lingered in Kessen's stoic shadow, and he wasn't budging. They were courteous, nodded as they walked by my kennel but never stopped to share events as they had in the past. I really missed their chats with me and never realized until now how much I missed being with them. I was lonely again and feeling a significant loss in my life.

He knows I'm here.

I worry about her decisions.

After replaying the events in my mind that led to this change in our friendship, I just don't see how it was my fault. I had a right to my own career choices just as they had a right to theirs. I actually understood their disappointment but not the effect on our relationship. At times, this sorority house life was just too baffling. Maybe my position as a subordinate member of the pack meant that I had no input whatsoever in the decision-making process. The pack leader had all of the power and control in order to maintain the integrity of the group, and I fully understood that. But, it was my belief that one's own life choices were personal and not at all pack-related. Apparently, that idea didn't go over too well with certain members of the pack.

Although I lacked my usual gusto, I still ran around the house whenever I had the opportunity because keeping in shape was necessary for my future plans. While I pretended not to see Kessen's judgmental glances as I flew back and forth through the halls, I still felt his disapproving eyes burning like lasers into the back of my head. Brightie gave me some impish looks now and then but still kept her distance. Her abiding by Kessen's wishes demonstrated the importance of his role as pack leader in the household. Surprisingly, I understood her compliance and respected his leadership position as well. I just didn't agree with his reluctance to accept free will in terms of career choices.

Mom sent me out into the yard to burn off some of my pent up energy since flying through the house like a stealth bomber wasn't acceptable. The yard, once mounded with drifting snow, was now a portrait of vivid colors and textures.

This yard makes me happy!

Lush green grass became the canvas for the various flowers that painted the yard. A variety of multi-colored day lilies dotted the perimeter while the pungent aroma of budding lilac bushes filled the air. Brighter shades of blues highlighted the huge Blue Spruce trees that now offered some relatively safe hiding places for occasional trespassing of birds, rabbits and squirrels. The Red Twig Dogwoods that completely lined the fence's perimeter were now filled with variegated leaves that no longer offered quite the danger of poking my eyes out. However, I was still very careful as I ran between the fence line and the bushes. Unlike their winter sparseness, the bushes now provided great hiding places for my make-believe intruders as well as a degree of eye safety. This yard, now radiant with nature's wonders, was certainly not the place for having sad feelings anymore.

With such beautiful sights and aromas in every direction, the yard was the perfect place to reflect on my past and plan for my future. The refreshing atmosphere of the colorful grounds left no room for my feeling down about missing Kessen and Brightie's companionship. It was in this awesome setting that I decided what I was going to do. While my decision probably wasn't the most acceptable choice, it was the best and only option for me: I was going back to being the sort of pup who came here months ago...a free spirit. Although I was alone now, I refused to be lonely anymore. To a great extent, "Operation Like Me" was a success; but starting today, it belonged to my past. The future belonged to me...one way or another. I needed no one when I first came here and didn't need anyone now. Having a new plan invigorated me, and I was ready to be the pup that I once was when I first arrived. Returning to the house with this renewed spirit was energizing and gave me hope for future escapades.

My bouncing into the house from the yard didn't go unnoticed by the folks. They were having company later in the day and expected all canines to be on their best behavior. When they saw my highly energetic entrance into the kitchen, their hopes regarding my being well-mannered were short lived. This newfound energy on my part made them change their current plans for my introduction to the guests. Not wanting to take any chances on my behavior, they confined me to the kitchen area where I might view the festivities through the rails of the kitchen gate. I still had a great view of the front door as well as easy access to my kennel in case I became over-stimulated by the arrival of the guests. My clever folks constantly thought of everything and were always two paws ahead of me.

The sound of the front doorbell ringing signaled the arrival of the guests. Kessen and Brightie quickly ran to their

I can see everything from here.

appointed throw rugs where all the formal greetings took place. They were like well-trained soldiers reporting quickly for sentry duty. If they had hands instead of paws, they would have saluted the guests as they entered. (*A dog just can't do a decent salute with a paw.*) If I had that kind of self-discipline and impulse control, I wouldn't be out here in the kitchen by myself. I'd be out there with the rest of the pack, sitting upright on a designated, colorful throw rug and practicing a very special salute. Perhaps, I'd even attempt to use my paw. If I accomplished such an incredible gesture, I would undoubtedly impress those special guests. Nevertheless, such an event was wishful thinking on my part since the kitchen was still my lookout post.

Colonel Kessen and Private Brightie (*my temporary nicknames for them*) greeted the guests appropriately and received numerous compliments for their behavior. Those super sentries just basked in the glow of the kind words, but

They are such good soldiers.

that feeling was fleeting since the guests then decided to visit me. That surely ticked off Colonel Kessen since he was still sitting on his throw rug waiting for more attention. Private Brightie, having closed her eyes during her greetings, didn't even realize that the guests had moved on to the kitchen. Needless to say, both dogs were astonished when they realized what had happened.

I was thrilled as well as taken aback by the attention of the guests. Even though they came as a group, the first woman was definitely the pack leader of the human guests. While diminutive in stature, her assertive approach conveyed absolute confidence which instantly identified her as the pack leader. Immediately intimidated by her demeanor as well as respect for her position in her pack, I assumed a submissive, sitting position. She was introduced as my Auntie Carol. From the moment I saw her smiling face, I knew that I had nothing to fear. Her squeals of joy as she lovingly scratched my head and ears filled my head and heart with warm, puppy fuzzies. In her eyes, I wasn't the Izz-Manian Devil or the Dust Demon. Instead, I was the most gorgeous pup that she had ever seen. Auntie Carol was both a perceptive pack leader as well as an extremely wise one. She was most assuredly my kind of human pack leader. If I were human, I'd be one of her staunch followers.

Then, I was introduced to my Cousin Carolyn, who had a dog named Riggins that she wanted me to meet some day. Cousin Steven was next and had two rabbits as pets. For obvious reasons, I probably wouldn't ever meet the rabbits, but I hoped to meet Riggins in the near future. My new friends actually got down on the floor in the kitchen and played with me for quite a while. I demonstrated my extraordinary retrieval techniques by fetching toys, giving them lots of puppy kisses and enjoying having them take turns scratching my tummy. I had such a wonderful time and hoped that our playing together would never end. Cousin Carolyn and Cousin Steven were mighty cool guests.

With all of this individual attention, a particular day that started out in such a dismal manner just got better and better. There was no room for feeling down anymore, and I still had another interesting guest to meet. Standing in the background was the last member of the human pack. However, being last to meet me didn't necessarily indicate her pack order. She had been patiently waiting for her turn to play with me and was introduced as my Auntie Fran. I reluctantly gave parting kisses to Cousin Carolyn and Cousin

Steven and assumed an appropriate greeting position for my next guest. As she entered my play area in the kitchen, my heart skipped a number of beats that not only startled me but took my breath away. If this physical reaction to Auntie Fran didn't cause an episode of reverse sneezing, then nothing would. At first I thought that I might be having some sort of medical emergency due to the over-exertion of playing. Fortunately, once I saw her cheerful expression and kind eyes, my heart rhythm gradually resumed its normal rate.

What was happening to me, and why did this newly

What's happening to me?

introduced guest cause me to respond so unusually? As she sat down on the floor with me, she put me in her lap and held me very close to her. I could actually feel her heart beating steadily as she gently scratched the underside of my neck. For the second time within a few minutes, my heart started rapidly skipping beats. Suddenly, I felt that special *tingle* in the pit of my stomach like the one I felt when I was with my birth mother…the one signifying her extreme love for me. This particular *tingle* of the moment wasn't just similar to hers…it was exactly the same in intensity and effect. While I felt some degree of enjoyable *tingle* with my new mom and dad, it wasn't the same as this powerful, comforting sensation. Who was this

Auntie Fran, and how could her holding me close to her heart duplicate the intense reaction as that of my birth mother?

This is getting scary!

I tried to control my breathing in order to avoid an episode of reverse sneezing which I often did when stressed but was met with little success. I was gasping for air while fighting the panic that was overwhelming me. With the help of Auntie Fran's comforting words and gentle stroking of my back, I resumed normal breathing and no longer felt alarmed. Instead, a degree of calmness settled over me like a blanket of warmth. Was it possible that my strong reaction to Auntie Fran's *tingle* was somehow meant to remind me of my birth mother's love? On the day that I was taken from my mother, she promised me that her love would always be with me to offer comfort and safety as long as I held her memory in my heart. I had forgotten her promise while making a new life for myself here in the sorority house. How could I have forgotten something so meaningful? Today, a day that started out filled with such loneliness, resulted in a much needed reminder of my birth mother's love. I owed it all to Auntie Fran's presence. Who would have thought that an intense feeling such as this particular *tingle* would mean so much to me? Words can't describe the warmth that filled my heart following this extraordinary occurrence. This day was such a lucky day for me...in more ways than one. I played with Auntie Fran for a while but knew that my time with her was limited. The intense *tingle* that I felt when with her did more for my spirits in one afternoon than all of the days that preceded it. I only wish that I were able to thank her for such a precious gift, but communication skills weren't my specialty...especially with humans.

Auntie Fran, Auntie Carol, Cousin Carolyn and Cousin Steven left later that day, but their visit made this day one of the best I ever had! I went to my kennel to relive the special experiences shared with my new friends. The kindness shown by them inspired me to look to the future with renewed enthusiasm. Thanks to Auntie Fran's presence, the rekindled thoughts and feelings of my birth mother's love will always remain in my mind and heart. There was great consolation in knowing that I'll never be alone again, and I owe it all to Auntie Fran. I sincerely hope that someday we'll meet again so I might find a way to thank her from the bottom of my heart. Because of her, my heart was no longer lonely…

I'll never be lonely again.

15

Stay The Course

As weeks passed, I followed through with my decision to behave like the pup who first arrived at the sorority house. I was a free spirit, cared only about myself and showed no signs of any behavioral improvements. In other words, I was a bit of a scamp. Running at full speed in the house and bouncing off closed doors was more of an expectation rather than an unexpected occurrence. While not as aloof as before and perhaps looking for some opportunity for compromise, Kessen and Brightie just watched me fly by in the halls without any intervention. The folks thought that I was going

If we don't move, she won't see us.

through my puppy adolescent stage...characterized by defiance and selective listening. They accepted my behaviors as some sort of rite of passage for pups and figured that they would just weather the storm until I came to my senses or outgrew that phase of canine development. Their acceptance of my dreadful behavior just reinforced my inability to make my feelings known to them. They were being understanding and unusually kind to me. In return, I was being a bratty pup, but I didn't know what else to do. If I could speak their language, my life would be so much easier.

The folks continued to teach me commands for the assistance program and took me out in public almost every day. My lack of conventional behavior continued while in public in the form of defiance and refusals. I was on the path of most resistance when in the public eye; and if that didn't get the folk's attention, nothing would. I just had to stay the course even though I hoped for another way to reach them, and being such an impish pup was not as much fun as it used to be. Once again, I was feeling that gravitational pull of the goodwill atmosphere practiced in the sorority house. Unfortunately, as effective as it was, it didn't alter my misbehavior.

The quiet rebellion to get play time restored to the Puppy Continuing class a few months ago gave me my inspiration for daily defiance techniques. Granted, I lost that previous battle, but I learned a most valuable lesson: Planning was the key to success in any endeavor...especially if it involved defiance.

I wasn't well-versed in rebellious techniques back then. Now, I was older and definitely wiser to the ways of the human world. I realized that when in public and wearing my cape, there were expectations of good behavior. That seemed like an easy feat for most pups, but I wasn't like most pups. I was willing to cooperate to an extent, but my calculated plan revolved around refusals and defiance.

At home when I saw my mom carrying the leash and cape, I would quickly withdraw to my kennel but was compliant when she put the cape on me and connected the leash. I walked willingly to the back door but then refused to leave. While they weren't impressive tactics by any means, they were still refusals; my ritual of "kennel-cape-leash-door" continued on a daily basis. Once in public, I walked nicely into any facility, responded appropriately to commands while either under a table in a restaurant or quietly sitting in an office waiting room. When it was time to leave, I hugged the floor in complete defiance of proper exit protocol. Knowing that the assistance organization's guidelines stressed positive reinforcement, I knew that dragging me from the establishment in front of people was not an option. Like a canine card game, I played the paw that I was dealt and gripped the floor until I decided to leave. (*My behavior was dreadful.*)

My folks were not at all pleased with my behavior and really didn't know why my actions changed so radically within the past few weeks. I wanted them to understand my motives but had no way of telling them. On the other paw, showing them my rebellious side wasn't working that well either. A huge part of me didn't like what I was doing to

This is a great hiding place.

them, but I had to find a way to communicate my needs…one way or another. If I complied with the rules of canine public etiquette, they would think that assistance to others was my goal in addition to theirs. In my mind, the defiant approach was the only way to get their attention. So, I didn't limit my refusals to restaurants and waiting rooms since I often refused to leave stores, malls, elevators, libraries and even hugged the middle of the street in defiance of appropriate walking. I often refused to exit the car even if food were placed in front of me.

A few weeks ago, Brightie, unintentionally, gave me some additional refusal techniques when she told me of Kessen's escapades of his youth. Little did she know that I would find a way to include those techniques in my outings. Between her information and my imagination, my unique tool box of defiance techniques was over-flowing.

I was just trying to help.

There were quite a few opportunities for defiance in public, but there were times that it did bother me because it distressed the folks. They meant well but didn't understand why I was doing all of this. Would they appreciate my misbehavior if they knew? Something told me that they wouldn't accept it on any terms. Was I now getting a conscience? Good grief! What was next?

In spite of the changes in my behavior, the folks continued to take me on public outings. They were either gluttons for public embarrassment or very determined puppy raisers. One day in particular, we were at a luncheon meeting, and my mom was asked to say a few words about our assistance organization. She was always willing to talk about the importance of assistance dogs. My dad sat at a table in the audience while I was situated in the cheap seats...under the table. (*What was wrong with that picture?*) Can't see a thing from the cheap seats. Anyway, as my mom talked, I was lulled by the rhythmic shifting of fringe on the tablecloth hanging in front of my face. Starting with a little lick and gradually building up to a slight nibble, I started slowly pulling on the tablecloth fringe. (*This was similar to Kessen's antics, but I took it to an art form!*) Each tug on the fringe brought the tablecloth closer and closer to me and was unintentionally pulling the silverware, dishes and glassware to the edge of the table. Because my dad was listening to my mom's words, he never noticed the corner of the tablecloth slowly being pulled from the tabletop.

Since all attention was on the speaker, no one noticed what I was doing...except my mom. While glancing at my dad for support, she saw the plates, silverware and glasses moving ever so slowly toward the end of the table. She immediately knew what I was doing and without skipping a beat asked my dad to stand with me and be introduced to the group. In doing so, she interrupted my pulling of the tablecloth from the table and avoided the embarrassment of my petulant behavior. Rather than draw attention to my mischief, she made several comments about me to the audience. First, she told them how very proud she was of me. Then, she went on to say that someday when training was completed and maturity kicked in, I would help someone in need. The audience applauded and made my earlier behavior seem ever so pathetic.

Mom unquestionably excelled at mind games. When would I ever learn? There was no contest...she was the best at those games and being second best only meant that I was no competition for her. I had to admit that my mom was a crafty one and anticipated many of my so-called adolescent moves. I really needed to foresee all possibilities in the future before engaging in misbehavior. She was, indeed, a masterful adversary.

There were many other opportunities for naughtiness within the next few months, but I gradually lost my zeal for them. The folks were still dismissing my misbehavior as part of canine development, and I didn't find much fun in doing them anymore. While those feelings didn't make me stop, the antics were fewer and farther between in terms of occurrence.

While at a church service one Sunday morning, a behavioral turning point occurred in my life. During the quietest part of the service, I unintentionally fell asleep with my head positioned on the kneeler in front of me. Ear-splitting snoring, characteristic of my sleep mode, followed and was suddenly interrupted by a noisy yawn. (*Brightie told me that Kessen often fell asleep in church and snored.*) All heads turned in the direction of the disruption. Not knowing that my folks had a potential assistance dog with them, the parishioners assumed that my dad was the perpetrator of the disturbance. Without skipping a beat, he apologized for the disruption and said that he just needed to focus on watching less television at night and getting more sleep before coming to church on Sunday. He assumed total blame for my rudeness, and if that's not an example of unconditional love than I don't know what is! The congregation just laughed at his response, and all was well. I remained blameless but nonetheless still felt remorse following the incident. Guilt was certainly a tricky result of misbehavior. Lately, it followed me around like a pesky fly.

That church service incident became the turning point for me in terms of putting an end to my naughtiness. Since being a free spirit wasn't helping my cause, I'd have to find another way to communicate my goals to my human and canine family. Getting support from Kessen and Brightie was the first and most difficult challenge since my dreams didn't coincide with their hopes for my future. Nevertheless, I definitely had to stay the course, but the course had to change in some ways. Restoring "Operation Like Me" through a joint spirit of compromise was one way to make that happen. Giving both the assistance and athletic worlds a chance might sway Kessen's and Brightie's opinions about my dreams. They, in turn, might give a little on their own, respond to my efforts and eventually accept my career choice. Anything was possible...

Compromise was the key to success.

In the spirit of change, striving for appropriateness in public was essential. The fundamental key to success in that endeavor was refraining from refusals and naughtiness. While I found a degree of delight in mischief, I had to forego that enjoyment in order for my plan to be successful. My athletic training, on the other paw, would continue on a daily basis...but only in the yard. As much as possible, I'd refrain from *zooming*, spinning, twirling and jumping in the house. Attempting changes in public and on the home turf wouldn't be easy, but I'd make every attempt to follow through on my part of the bargain. By showing Kessen and Brightie that I was both eager and willing to compromise, they, in turn, might be willing to cooperate and help me. According to my plan, rebellion and mischievous antics were actions of the past. Compromise was the promising, new game in town and, in my opinion, was the path to future success. Nothing would stop me now…

There's no stopping me now.

16

Settle The Score

Attempting to end my mischievous antics with the folks while in public was just the first step in getting back on track with the friendly vibes of the sorority house. That objective was easier said than done because I had followed a pattern of rebellious tactics for such a long time that complete reversal of my mischief was extremely challenging. The temptation to hug the pavement while on walks or the appeal of refusing to leave a public place frustrated my intent to end my misbehavior. Realizing that naughtiness was somewhat amusing to me made reversal of mischief even more difficult, but I was determined to beat that dreadful habit. It would just take time, and I had five more months before being shipped away to Advanced Training in order to make that happen.

While I relapsed into mischief now and then, the path of appropriate behavior was becoming easier as the weeks passed. The folks even noticed the change in my behavior and imparted lavish praise following each instance of good conduct. Because of my behavioral improvements in public, they even played ball with me in the yard in the evening. I was quick to show them my spinning, twirling and parallel jumping skills while attempting to catch the ball thrown through the air. Maybe they would catch on to my desire to be a disc dog by my doing these unusual things. My dad wondered why I didn't just run after the ball instead of doing so many aerobatic movements. Apparently, my demonstrative clues, while spectacular to watch, were very far from informative. Nevertheless, as my behavior

I love playing in the yard.

improved in public, more yard time was given to demonstrate my disc dog skills. All in all, I felt pretty good about myself even though no one seemed to get what I was attempting to do with my airborne antics. My inability to communicate with them in their language was, indeed, a major barrier to my success.

While progressing in terms of public behavior was promising, attempts at home were not as successful. Without people watching me, I didn't feel the need to behave as much. Without an audience, there was no risk for reprisals other than time outs in the kennel. So I continued to periodically *zoom* through the house as well as utilize my "kennel-cape-leash-door" refusal tactic. After all, I practiced refusals for months and couldn't just turn that around in a short period of time. Anything worth doing took time and effort. While not totally successful with changing my misbehavior, I felt that I had made some positive strides in that direction with my mom and dad.

The greater challenge was to settle the score once and for all with Kessen. Winning him over to my beliefs in a way that would not compromise his standing in the pack was the key to success, and respecting his position as pack leader was essential in getting back into his good graces. Up until now, I was the rebellious one who flipped my paw at every form of conformity within the pack, and that resistance to compliance made me an outsider. Even the neighborhood dogs recognized my lack of status and were, at times, aloof toward me. The canine community is such a tight group.

Truth be told, I desperately needed to work my way back into the pack, but getting back into Kessen's good graces was not going to be easy. I might only get one shot at making things right between us. That endeavor had to be well planned and unexpected since the element of surprise was my greatest chance for success. Now, I just had to figure out a way to accomplish my goal.

Surprisingly, an opportunity for settling the score came about without any deliberation on my part. Not having any input into the situation probably worked in my favor since my plans rarely worked. (*That was such a harsh but accurate commentary on my success ratio.*) It came without warning in the form of a puppy visiting the sorority house for the weekend. Kessen and Brightie were already prepared for her visit and found appropriate hiding places. As usual, I didn't have a clue as to what was happening. At first, seeing the lowered food and water bowls placed in the corner along with a smaller wire kennel didn't jar my memory at all. Then I remembered that those smaller items were used when I was just a pup and first came to the sorority house. Either I was being put on smaller rations and evicted from my kennel in lieu of a smaller one, or we were getting a visitor for the weekend…a visitor of puppy proportions.

Fortunately, my living arrangements and daily rations were not changing. Instead, I was right about the visitor…a pup named Tansy was coming to visit. Her name conjured up thoughts of a sweet, gentile pup of high class upbringing, and I couldn't wait to meet her. She arrived Friday evening and would be our guest until Sunday afternoon. At first sight of her, she looked exactly like me when I was a pup. She had an ebony coat that hugged her body like an elastic sock and gave the impression that she didn't have an ounce of fat on her puppy body. Her sparkling white baby teeth were sharp as needles, and her perpetual energy level rivaled, if not surpassed, mine when I was her age. If Kessen and Brightie thought that I had issues with conformity, they had an awakening facing them with events of this coming weekend. She definitely lived up to her Labrador Retriever reputation. Compared to me, she was jet-propelled!

She looks sweet, doesn't she?

Our first meeting with Tansy was a bit chaotic. It started out well with Kessen and Brightie, being the A Team, meeting her first and doing the appropriate welcoming gestures of sniffing body parts. Rather than reciprocate, Tansy's method of greeting was to jump on each of them as much as she could. She jumped, circled, pounced and even ran under their chests while they stood. Brightie's eyeballs rolled around in their sockets in order to keep track of Tansy. Yet, throughout all of the jumping, bobbing and weaving, Kessen just stood perfectly still. Tansy was just a pup and really didn't know any better, but Kessen, feeling that his position as pack leader was being disrespected, decided to leave the area. Brightie, of course, followed in his paw steps as her eyeballs gradually returned to the normal position in their sockets.

The folks then brought in the B Team…that would be me. I did the ritualistic greeting while expecting the same jumping treatment from Tansy, but she surprised me. She returned my sniffing in an appropriate manner and returned my play bow. Just when I felt a sense of pride since I accomplished what Kessen couldn't, she jumped all over, around and under me like a flea on an unprotected dog. She was as relentless as her energy was limitless. I quickly ran to the safety of my kennel and burrowed myself into the farthest corner. I knew that she could still see me but hoped that she wouldn't breach my property line. This was going to be some eventful weekend. Being the B Team was one tough gig!

Our exercise and play time came much sooner than anticipated. Because Kessen and Brightie were older, weighed quite a bit more than our visitor and played a bit rougher, it was decided that Tansy and I would play in the yard together. Once again, I drew the short treat from the treat jar. (*Thanks folks.*) I outweighed Tansy by at least thirty pounds but was the better match for play time than the older dogs. At first, we ran around a bit and hid behind some bushes and shrubs, but then the direction of the play changed. Tansy turned her sights on me like a laser beam, and her pursuit of me was unrelenting. I attempted every hiding place I could find, but she always found me and jumped all over me until I ran to another hiding place. Seeing her merciless pursuit of me and the unmistakable pleading for help in my eyes, mom and dad brought out some toys for her. While those toys kept Tansy from jumping all over me for a little while, the interest in the stuffed squeak-toys was short lived. Why go for inert toys when a living and breathing dog was up front and personal in the play yard? Once again, that dog would be me. She was unwavering in her jumping up, over, under and around while I attempted to avoid her antics. Insistent on scaling my back at all costs, Tansy was like a mountain climber aiming for worldly prestige by reaching the summit of some mountain top. What gave her the idea that my back was her pinnacle of success?

For the record, I was slowly losing my calm and welcoming demeanor. I glanced around the yard for some well-needed assistance and saw that Kessen and Brightie were watching the action from the sunroom windows. While my total pathetic look begged help from them, I saw that they were actually smiling at the goofy actions of the weekend visitor. Getting help from them was not going to happen today. (*That's what happens to outsiders!*) They were stuck in the sunroom and were pretty smug about that situation. However, pretty soon being confined to that room would be a detriment to them, and the last laugh might very well be mine.

They are definitely laughing at me.

The situation took a definite reversal when Tansy remembered seeing a colorful, ring toy in a basket by the closet door as we went out to play. Earlier, on our way to the yard, she asked me about that toy since it was not with the regular toys. I told her that it was Kessen's special toy and under no circumstances was it to be touched by any dog in the pack. I also reminded her that Kessen was the pack leader, and his wishes were to be respected at all times. I had my hind legs crossed behind my back when I said that since I didn't want Tansy to know that I wasn't always as respectful as I led her to believe.

Tansy, being a young pup, untrained in appropriate pack behavior and bored with scaling my back wanted to play with that ring toy now more than ever. I warned her again about not disrespecting Kessen's position by grabbing his ring toy, but she was undaunted. She ran from the yard, through the dog run, onto the deck area, into the kitchen and grabbed that ring toy from the basket. Once it was in her mouth, she ran from room to room until she reached the yard again.

Kessen had seen her interest in his ring toy from his position in the house and hoped that she wouldn't dare disrespect him by playing with it. As she grabbed the toy from the basket, Kessen's eyes could only follow her from room to room and window to window since he was confined to the sunroom. She had his toy, and he was unable to stop her. His only alternative was to watch her repeatedly fling his precious ring toy up into the air while he was confined to the

How dare she grab my ring toy?

sunroom. Let me just say that he wasn't smiling anymore. (*Payback was such a hoot!*)

186

From my vantage point in the yard, I watched this snatch and grab of the ring toy played out as if in slow motion. I saw Kessen following Tansy's movements as he watched her from the windows of each of the rooms leading to the yard and not being able to do anything to stop it. This was my unexpected opportunity to get back into his good graces, and I was ready to do the right thing.

As Tansy raced into the yard from the dog run with Kessen's ring toy held high on her head, she ran around the yard in a zigzag pattern so as to avoid being caught by me. I raced after her, but she was a lot faster than I anticipated. That no-ounce-of-fat body of hers did her justice as I pursued her. Every attempt to corner her led to her escaping through the lilac bushes, running under the Blue Spruce trees or hiding behind the Burning Bushes. This little pup ran liked greased lightning and definitely knew how to avoid being caught!

Since my chances of catching Tansy in the huge yard were slim to none, I decided to change my tactics. Remembering Linus' Three Step Action Plan for appropriate canine behavior, I figured that I might just tweak it a bit to regain Kessen's toy. Slowly approaching her in a non-threatening manner, I got her attention by curling up in the grass and totally ignoring her. She was cautiously intrigued by my lack of interest in the toy debacle and decided to come closer. As she slowly approached while carrying that ring toy in her mouth, I controlled my initial impulse to rip that thing from her mouth. If I ripped Kessen's toy while attempting to retrieve it for him, she and I would both be in trouble. So, I continued to ignore her until she came so close to me that I saw my reflection in her eyes.

Using Linus' process as my plan, my first step was to curl my lip to get her attention. Since she gave me an odd look, I added the next step which was a menacing, low growl and still no response from Tansy. Next, came the muffled snap in her direction. If that didn't work, perhaps nothing would. Linus' Three Step Action Plan of lip quiver, low growl and muffled snap was complete. Theoretically, she should now be ready to comply with my request to drop Kessen's toy.

Once again, a plan of mine went awry, or so she thought. The look on her face was that of total amusement. This young whippersnapper of a pup was laughing at me and my attempts to win favor with Kessen by redeeming his cherished ring toy. Where was her respect for her elders as well as her position as a guest in the sorority house? While her name conjured up thoughts of class and proper upbringing, her actions were far from acceptable canine behavior.

Pretending to have lost in my attempts to retrieve Kessen's ring toy, I acquiesced to her having the toy and gave her a nod of approval. She approached me while holding that prized ring toy with the look of success in her eyes. I allowed her a brief moment to believe that she had undermined an older dog, but then added my tweaked Fourth Step to Linus' process. While she flaunted her success, I took her completely off guard by body-blocking her with a quick, unsuspecting move, snarled uncontrollably and added some erratic actions that implied extreme, mental instability on my part. Because my demeanor caused her fear and confusion, I grabbed that ring toy from her mouth and took off in the yard. Being much stronger and already having my adult teeth, I was able to extricate the trophy from her mouth without even loosening any of her baby teeth. Seeing my angry expression as I gripped the toy caused her to quickly retreat behind the shrubbery. Who was the tough one now? She didn't know that I was really just pretending to be angry and putting on a show for Kessen. I wasn't capable of being that angry...not by a long shot, and surprisingly, a plan of mine actually worked.

I secured his toy.

Turning to face Kessen's gaze in the sunroom, I did a courteous play bow, assumed a respectful sitting position on my haunches and dropped the ring toy in front of Kessen's gaze. As he looked through the sunroom window, Kessen saw that I had freed his precious toy from the visitor and, in doing so, honored him as the pack leader. Hopefully, that meant something to him in terms of welcoming me back into his good graces.

Tansy and I were then called into the house and into our respective kennels. Kessen and Brightie were let out into the yard where Kessen reclaimed his prized ring toy. Brightie just danced around him knowing the significance of my actions that led to rescuing his ring toy. I was definitely back in the good graces of the pack, and it was all because of Tansy.

Tansy was our weekend warrior.

Tansy was only with us for the weekend, but she was instrumental in my being welcomed back into Kessen's good graces. It was strange that her inappropriate behavior led to my re-admittance into the pack which entitled me to all the wonderful opportunities the pack offered. Tansy was, without a doubt, a weekend blessing, and she learned two valuable lessons: Never, and I mean never...touch Kessen's ring toy and by no means mess with the B Team. Definitely words of wisdom to live by...

Today I saved his precious toy.

17

No Looking Back

In addition to receiving praise and extra yard time from the folks for good behavior, I realized that encouragement came in many unexpected ways as well. While I had been in training for assistance during the past ten months, I never encountered a dog who was actually in a service position…until today. The event was a fund raiser for the assistance organization that sponsored me, and the folks were in charge of an information booth while I greeted people as they walked past. There were quite a few family pets at the fund raiser along with dogs representing various forms of assistance. There were service dogs for individuals in wheel chairs and returning veterans, dogs for the hearing impaired, seizure response dogs, guide dogs for the blind and many others.

As I scanned the crowds, I saw this magnificent, yellow Labrador Retriever wearing an assistance cape approaching our booth with his partner. The pride in his service position was demonstrated by his confident stride and watchful care for the safety of his partner. As they approached our booth, I couldn't wait to hear about his experiences as well as share my dreams with him.

This remarkable-looking service dog was named Deon. He worked in a helping situation for the last eight years and

Deon was very understanding.

loved every minute of it. After hearing about his experiences and love for his service career, I was a bit reluctant to share my career plans with him. However, he insisted on hearing about my future goals since it was evident by my wearing the cape that I was already involved in training for some type of assistance.

Imagine his surprise when I told him about my dreams of athletic championships, trophies, ribbons and awards. He took a few minutes to absorb my thoughts and then gave me his feedback. Deon had some interesting challenges to my way of thinking. He understood that not all dogs wanted to be of assistance to others. Of the numerous dogs who wanted that career, some would not be capable of success. Service to others was a challenging but rewarding career choice. Deon also cautioned me to be careful of my decisions because sometimes dreams that came true had elements of disappointment and regret. (*What a downer that part of the conversation turned out to be!*) However, his observations probably impacted my views as well as added doubts about my goals more than any dog had so far. Even Kessen's logic wasn't as good as Deon's.

Because of Deon's values and beliefs, I felt a newfound respect for a career in assistance which is probably why his words made such an impression. Deon believed that service, along with the bond he shared with his partner, was his greatest reward and one that he experienced on a daily basis. The cape that distinguished him as a service dog was his trophy that he wore with pride, and it held more significance than any ribbons or awards. He sure gave me a lot to think about in ways that were special. I didn't have the nerve to tell him that I had been hiding from wearing my cape for the last ten months while in training. What was I thinking? Were ribbons and trophies more important than a daily reminder of helping others? It certainly sounded like it, but that was definitely going to change. I was going to start paying more attention to wearing my cape and not hide from it so often...which was probably the right things to do. After all, I was an assistance dog in training even though I wasn't sure about the assistance part.

After hearing about Deon's experiences as well as his words of wisdom, I found myself rethinking my goals making me somewhat torn between what had been my life's dreams and what I might be missing if I didn't give an assistance career a chance. Not only was I changing my behavior, but in some ways, I was also altering my thoughts regarding career choices. Something was happening to me in terms of my thoughts and actions, and I wasn't sure if I liked it or not.

How could my lifelong athletic dreams be shifting in such an extreme direction? This conflict of career direction was all too puzzling for me, and I only had five more months left at the sorority house to make the right decision for my future. The pressure was building with each passing day.

As if I weren't confused enough, my second experience with assistance dogs came the following week at a dog walk meant to raise funds for disabled individuals. There were all different breeds of dogs present for the fund raiser, but the most prominent dogs were the ones involved with helping careers. Recognized by their signature capes and devotion to their partners, there were two special dogs who stood out in the crowd.

Service was her priority.

The first was Kelyna...a sleek, caramel-colored Golden Retriever who was a service dog for the hearing impaired. While her stunning appearance sparked some interest, her devotion to her partner and attentiveness to her service job were what drew people to her. I was captivated by her charm, dedication to her job and ballerina-like prance as she walked slightly ahead of her partner to be on the alert for sounds.

We spent some time sharing experiences although I didn't dwell on my months of refusals. She understood my conflicting career choices and wasn't one to judge. She shared that as a young pup, she had some definite career conflicts.

In addition to her assistance training, she loved to dance to music. Her puppy raiser named Jan, who lived in North Carolina and happened to be friends with my folks, was a certified dog trainer. Jan had all sorts of unique techniques for training. Canine freestyle dancing was one of Jan's unique ways of teaching obedience, technique and coordination of movements. Kelyna loved being swept away by the sounds and the strategic movements of the dance. At times, she even thought a theatrical dance career was in her future. However, canine freestyle dancing was only one aspect of Kelyna's training. While she loved that part of it, the lure of assistance to others was much greater for her. So, Kelyna went on to be a service dog for the hearing impaired and never looked back on her potential dancing opportunities. She was, after all, where she belonged and loved every aspect of her career.

I was so impressed with Kelyna's story that she gave up her love of dancing in lieu of service to others. Might I be willing to do the same in terms of giving up athletic fame in exchange for assistance? I certainly wasn't sure of that possibility at this point in my life, but what I suddenly realized was that I was actually considering it. Months ago, it wouldn't have been a consideration. Yet at this point in my life, those thoughts were causing interference with my original goals of athletic glory.

Time passed ever so quickly following my conversations with Kelyna as people stopped by our booth for information and greetings from me. Then, the dog walk began, and all the various breeds marched energetically through the park with their handlers. It was quite the sight to see. In the midst of the walkers, I spotted a striking English Golden Retriever wearing an assistance cape and suddenly realized that I knew her. It was Carlita…the dog that I met a few months ago while at a seminar for assistance pups in training. At that time, she and her puppy raiser named Jan, who also raised Kelyna, gave demonstrations as to the proper teaching of commands as well as discussing the public demands of a working dog. Judging by her formal assistance cape and partner, Carlita was successful not only in her rigorous time in Advanced Training but with her placement as an assistance dog. Way to go, Carlita!

By keeping my eyes on Carlita's cape, I was able to keep track of her in hopes of some meet and greet time following the event. Perhaps we could share experiences just as I had shared experiences with Kelyna the week before this event. While I hadn't seen her since she was young, seeing Carlita in a successful, service career was awe inspiring. As luck would have it, her partner was friends with my folks, and he eagerly approached our booth with Carlita. He was very handsome in human terms, and both were so perfectly matched since Carlita's appearance was stunning. What a great team they made!

Beauty fades…service is forever.

After sharing numerous stories with Carlita, I was more confused than ever. She described her life of service as so fulfilling but didn't judge my choice in terms of an athletic career as opposed to one of assistance to others. According to her, my future was up to me, and no one else could make that decision for me. Not only was this dog utterly remarkable in appearance, but she was incredibly wise as well.

Talking to Carlita and Kelyna today, as well as sharing experiences with Deon the week before, gave me so much to think about in terms of choices. Each dog seemed so accomplished and fulfilled by their careers, and there was no looking back for them. Deon was right when he said that his position as a service dog was more than enough of a reward for him on a daily basis. Both Kelyna and Carlita shared the same views and had such pride in their chosen careers.

I certainly had to rethink my goals while I still had the opportunity as well as the choice. Part of me still longed for the championship glory of trophies, ribbons and awards. Nevertheless, that nagging thought of assistance to others kept creeping up into my brain. That evening, as my dad had me jumping, twirling and spinning for that thrown ball in the yard, I would lose myself in the motions and not think of anything else. I just wanted to clear my mind, be free of any decision making and enjoy the splendor of floating through the air after that ball. There would be time for life's decisions, but tonight was not the night...

18

Get Busy

The weeks following the fund raisers and meetings with the service dogs just flew by. As a result of my somewhat improved behavior, I was getting a lot more yard time. The folks had stepped up my assistance training since I only had a few more months left with them, but the improvements I made in terms of behavior were most appreciated by them. Even Kessen and Brightie noticed the changes, and my position in the pack definitely improved with each passing day.

An amazing event took place one day after playing with my dad in the yard. He repeatedly threw this rubber ball into the air while I jumped as high as I could, spun around and attempted to grab it in midair. It always dropped on the ground before I caught it, but my timing and techniques were getting better. Catching a ball wasn't the same as I imagined catching a disc would be, but it was better than nothing. My dad still didn't understand why I went through all of these motions just to catch a ball when all I really had to do was run after it. Because I was behaving in public, he wasn't going to rock the doghouse trying to find out. Besides, he was just grateful that my *zooming* in the house wasn't as frequent, and I willingly left public places rather than hug the floor while refusing to leave. All in all, I was earning a pretty good reputation in terms of my house and public behavior.

This particular day, Kessen and Brightie were watching my twirling around while I was jumping for the thrown ball.

Izzy makes us laugh!

Kessen had a front row seat and sat with his prized ring toy that I so forcefully rescued from Tansy's grasp a few weeks ago. Brightie positioned herself under the maple tree and enjoyed my twirling show while crunching on a dried twig found near the fragrant lilac bushes. Running, jumping and spinning took a lot of energy. Pretty soon, I was ready to go back to my kennel for a well-deserved rest. My dad led all three of us into the house, and I immediately went into my kennel, curled up in the corner and slept for a while.

In the midst of a dream about championship glory, I was suddenly awakened and pulled from my dream state by my name being called. Brushing off the fog of dreamland, I realize it was the sound of Brightie summoning me to the sun room for an immediate audience with Kessen. What did I do now? Not knowing what I had done wrong and not wanting to jeopardize my position in the pack, I rushed through the kitchen to the sunroom. Due to my excessive speed, I slid on the ceramic tiles into the sunroom and came muzzle to muzzle with Kessen who was holding a circular object in his mouth. (*Just great! He's got another prized possession that I'll have to rescue some day!*) I was so close to him that I could see my reflection in his eyes, and I must admit that I looked mighty apprehensive. After all, one doesn't get summoned by the leader of the pack every day.

Strangely, Kessen didn't even blink as I almost skidded into him. Once I regained my composure, I took a respectful

This is a very special gift.

paw-step back from his muzzle and assumed an appropriate and respectful sitting position. That was when I recognized what Kessen held so gently in his mouth…that circular object in his mouth was a colorful disc. Where in the world did Kessen get a disc? Was he leading a covert life as a disc dog? If so, how was it kept a secret? I'd never even seen him jump for food let alone for a flying disc. No…that couldn't be it. Being a disc dog really necessitated an abundance of energy, and the most energy Kessen ever expended was getting to his food bowl before the other pack members. This sure was quite a peculiar situation, and I was clearly at a loss as to what to do.

As Brightie watched from the doorway, I wasn't sure what was going on or what was about to happen to me. Kessen maintained his stoic stance and still didn't blink his eyes. That "eye thing" alone was creepy in addition to being intimidating, but why was he holding that disc in his mouth? Was he taunting me because he knew that being a disc dog was one of my dreams? If so, there was nothing I could do about it since he was the pack leader and had the upper paw.

As I sat directly in front of him with a puzzled expression on my face, Kessen did the unexpected. He dropped the disc at my front paws and told me that the disc was his gift to me for the positive changes in my behavior. Watching my actions during the past weeks, he recognized that I gave both the assistance as well as the athletic worlds a chance. Due to my efforts, he wanted to reward me in the best possible way.

She needs to follow her dreams.

The moment got even better when Kessen mentioned that he was proud of me. If I chose athletic glory instead of assistance, he wouldn't stand in my way. The disc was special in that it was given to him by a group of school children following a most successful fund raiser for the disabled. By giving it to me, he was granting permission for me to follow my dreams. While I was overwhelmed by the gesture, his expression of pride in my behavior actually meant more than receiving the disc. Nevertheless, I was ready to take that disc out of retirement and get some good use out of it. No more twirling around for a tiny rubber ball when I had the right tool within my paws. I couldn't wait to get out into the yard and practice. As it turned out, I was about to get busy with the real deal...

19

Out Of Reach

From the moment Kessen dropped that disc at my paws, I knew that my dreams were coming true. Now, I had the ideal tool to advance my jumping and whirling techniques. Gripping that disc for the first time and feeling the raised, plastic ridge that secured it against my teeth was such an awesome feeling. I couldn't wait to take it out to the yard and work on my routine. Unfortunately, I wasn't able to go out in the evening because it had rained, and the grass was very slippery. As anxious as I was to toss that disc into the air, I'd have to wait until tomorrow. But, just to be sure this wasn't all a dream, I brought that disc into my kennel for the night and used it as my very own plastic pillow. I wasn't supposed to have any toys in the kennel, but my mom made an exception this time and allowed it. That disc didn't make a very comfortable pillow, but I wasn't taking any chances with my precious new gift.

The next day, my public responsibilities seemed to take forever. In spite of my impatience to get back to my newly acquired gift, I was very well behaved. I wasn't taking any chances since misbehavior might take away my yard time. The folks and I first went to the local coffee shop where I spent some time in the cheap seats again…under the table.

But, I wasn't complaining about the seating arrangements. I was behaving appropriately and even left the premises without any prodding or pleading. My folks thought I was a very different dog lately and were very pleased with the changes in my behavior. Following our stop at the coffee shop, we visited a library, practiced greetings with some children and finally made our way back to the house. Truth be told, I really had a good time with this assistance gig, and in terms of a future, it definitely had its advantages. (*I never thought I'd say that!*) However, all I thought about was working with that treasured disc.

When we finally got home, Kessen and Brightie were waiting for me at the back door because they knew how anxious I was to try out my disc. As the door opened, I gave a quick nod to them and quickly scampered into the kitchen to get that treasured object. There it was, my plastic pillow, in its total splendor pushed against the corner of my kennel. It was a glorious sight to behold, but gawking at it wasn't going to get me into the yard any faster. I grabbed that disc and bolted through the kitchen, the sunroom, the dog run and finally entered the yard. Kessen grabbed his ring toy, and Brightie snatched a squeak ball from the toy box as they followed in my paw steps to the yard. They found suitable vantage points for viewing the exhibition in the yard and awaited my initiation into the disc dog world.

Having an audience for my inaugural jump was a bit stressful, but I had been practicing my jumps and spins for months. I was confident that as soon as I launched that disc, I'd give them quite a show. As Kessen gave me a nod to begin the show, I tossed that disc, locked my eyes on the target and jumped as high as I could to catch it. Midway through the jump, I realized that I had forgotten to spin around while airborne. It all went so fast that while I was thinking of all of the maneuvers, the disc dropped to the ground. Well, everyone deserved a practice jump, and that one was mine. Once again, I tossed that disc into the air, focused my eyes on it and twirled around. In my excitement to do it properly, I forgot to jump and actually just spun around on the grass as the disc landed by my paws. This endeavor wasn't as easy as I thought it would be and was becoming quite frustrating.

By this time, my audience had grown. Sammy sat patiently on the other side of the fence, Kaiser left his sentinel post in the front yard to watch, and Finnegan was impatiently pacing back and forth while waiting for the show to begin. To top that off, the folks, looking out the window and seeing the neighborhood dogs gathered around the fence, came out to the yard to see what was happening. Once the folks saw what was going on, they applauded and cheered while I made a few more attempts. Sadly, I failed to catch any of my disc tosses. What was I doing wrong? Feeling like a complete failure from the numerous unsuccessful attempts, I just sat in the grass next to that disc with my tongue hanging out. Having that gift was supposed to be the answer to my future, and all I had now was the scrutiny of my audience.

There was some laughter from the Finnegan side of the fence, but the others quite understood my predicament. Sammy said that I just needed practice, and Kaiser reminded me that he couldn't even jump into the air let alone catch a disc. Kessen and Brightie just encouraged me to keep trying and not give up on my dreams of future glory.

As I sunk lower into the grass, my dad came to my rescue with unexpected but useful information that saved me from further embarrassment. He picked up the disc from the grass and explained that I wasn't successful because he, himself, wasn't doing his part. I wasn't supposed to do the tossing…he was! That's why I couldn't catch that flying disc. (*Now, I don't wish to sound ungrateful, but my dad might have told me sooner!*) Anyway, he had me go out a few paw steps in front of him and focus on the disc. He launched that disc into the air, and I seized the opportunity for success. With my eyes locked precisely on the target, I jumped into the air and actually caught it. (*Gotcha!*) As I landed on the ground with

What a glorious moment!

that disc in my mouth, I witnessed the pride in my dad's face and realized how very grateful I was for his assistance. He not only saved me from my perceived failure but gave me my future in the first toss of the precious disc. The audience cheered me on as I attempted the next toss, and I even added a twirl to the maneuver. Once again, I was successful and owed it all to my dad's help. I'd still be out in the yard tossing that disc up in the air and missing it if not for my dad's intervention. Gotta love that guy! Gotta love him a lot!

My dad saved the day.

During the next few days, my wonderful dad and I practiced every day with that special disc. I was extremely skilled in terms of catching it but not as successful in terms of gaining height and twirling around while airborne. I used to be so good at those aspects of high jumping. As a young puppy, I was able to spin around while jumping higher than any pup in the kennel. When I came to the sorority house, I soared higher than ever. I used to leap so high that I could see Sammy on the other side of the fence when I was airborne. Now, I barely reached the tips of the bushes. What was happening to me?

Go see for yourself.

Sammy was always my source of logical explanations, so I approached him about my dilemma. He knew that I had difficulty with reaching heights in my jumps but didn't want to say anything unless asked. Sammy was never one to dwell on lengthy explanations; he always went directly to the marrow of the dog bone…even if painful. He told me to go through the dog run and take a good look at myself in the glass patio doors on the deck. When I did that, I would finally know precisely what my problem was.

His suggestion seemed like a very strange thing for me to do, but Sammy has never given me bad advice. Trusting in his suggestion, I went off to take a look at my reflection in the glass. Much to my surprise, there was a huge, stunning Labrador Retriever looking back at me. Priding myself in being athletically inclined, I never put much thought into what I looked like. Nevertheless, this dog looking back at me was awesome in both appearance and stature. What did Sammy want me to discover?

It was in that moment that I realized why Sammy sent me to view my reflection. I was no longer that little, agile puppy with long, lanky legs and weighing about fifteen pounds. Looking back at me in the glass was an adult dog weighing at least fifty pounds more than when I first arrived here. No wonder I couldn't reach those great heights anymore. I had grown up and was powerfully built. Being a light-weight wasn't part of my breed's make-up. (*Was I always the last one to learn important details?*) I'd never be able to jump competition heights because of my weight. For that reason alone, my dream of disc dog glory was out of reach. The realization that I trained and worked so hard for something that was totally out of my reach from the very beginning of my life was devastating for me. I truly wanted to take some consolation in the fact that I had at least tried my best, but I just couldn't find the courage to feel that way right now. The disappointment was just too overwhelming.

Lost in my thoughts of what might have been or could have been, I looked back at my past decisions. In hindsight, I gave up the idea of being a dock diving dog because the thought of diving into a huge pool of deep water wasn't at all appealing to me. Once I saw how big that pool was, I decided against that activity. However, that decision was entirely my own. Now, I had no choice in the matter and had to face another disappointment in terms of future goals. Not having the option of being a disc dog after all of my dreams, hard work and training made it all the more disappointing.

I went back into the yard and thanked Sammy for his advice even though it caused this huge gap in my future plans. Kessen watched from the corner of the yard but never approached me. He knew that I was hurting and had to sort things out for myself...which was a very different reaction for him. Apparently, I wasn't the only one who had changed. Kessen now believed that as an adult dog, career decisions were mine to make and not governed by the pack leader...big changes for both of us.

As I went back into the house holding my disc, I passed my reflection on the way in and just shook my head in disbelief. While I definitely looked amazing, I felt saddened by the events of the day. On the way to my kennel, I no longer felt the need to sleep with my disc. It had lost its significance in terms of my dreams, so I just tossed it into my toy box. While I still valued it as a special gift from Kessen, I never played with it again...

Sometimes a dream is just a dream.

20

Moving On

I moped around for a few days following the end of my disc dog dream, but Kessen and Brightie encouraged me to move on with my career options. So what if I chose not to be a dock diving dog because I didn't want to jump into a huge pool of water or wasn't able to be a disc dog because of my size and weight. It wasn't the end of the world, and I certainly had a lot more going for me. I had my family, friends, newly discovered good looks, a valued appreciation of assistance work and other career choices as well. I was good to go but still lost myself for a few days in a pity party. As in every one of my past pity parties, I was the only guest in attendance.

While I sulked around for a while, my mom noticed that I just wasn't myself. I wasn't eating with my usual gusto and lacked my normal spunky attitude. While she didn't know the real cause for my sadness, she knew that I was either ill or something had gone very wrong in my life. Seeing the treasured disc relegated to the toy box was an additional clue for her, but she didn't know why I had tossed it there. Mom knew that I loved that disc and even slept with it in my kennel for a while. Now it was just another toy in the toy box. At this moment, it would have been a good time for her to be able to speak my language or for me to be able to speak hers, but I knew that wasn't going to happen. While I wallowed in self-pity, my mom had plans of her own for me.

In spite of the language barrier between us, my mom always came up with some practical solution to a problem. Since I wasn't eating very much and was a bit lethargic, she took me to the veterinarian to rule out any physical problem. Once I was deemed healthy by the veterinarian, she deferred to her Plan B which was destined to shake off my melancholy mood. In her mind, all I needed was something to lift my spirits. What did this wonderful person come up with? A play date! The wheels were set in motion for that event, but I didn't know when, where or if it would ever take place.

Two days later, while still in a moping mood, I decided to change my usual routine and sleep later. Because I was typically an early riser, sleeping late was a rare event for me. In view of the fact that continued sulking was my only plan for the day, I did just that. Had I followed my usual routine as an early riser, I would have noticed the goings-on in the yard. By sleeping beyond my regular wake-up time, I really missed a lot.

A few hours later, my mom and dad encouraged me to come out to the yard. Kessen and Brightie were waiting for me and seemed to be blocking my view of the area. Seeing their happy faces brought a smile to mine. As they moved off to the side, I was able to see what they were hiding. The first thing I noticed was the water-filled baby pool strategically located under the maple tree. As a pup, Kessen thought that pool was a huge water bowl placed in the yard for his refreshment during the hot summer months. Knowing the history of that pool just made me laugh, and I already felt better.

Off to the left of the pool and stretched across a length of grass was a long tunnel...opened on each end. It looked like an enormous worm just waiting for someone or something to venture through its openings. At first, I was intrigued by it but then caught a glimpse of the rest of the yard. In addition to the tunnel, there were single, double and triple jumps of varying heights strategically placed in between a tire jump which is just a tire suspended closely to the ground by two poles. A colorful seesaw was positioned in the middle, and completing the course were the weave poles. The individual poles were positioned in a straight line and had equal spacing between each pole. Dogs have to weave their way between the poles, and it is quite a complicated maneuver depending on the size of the dog. Small dogs travel around the poles with great speed and ease. Larger dogs have to shift their bodies around each pole as they move around them. While that makes it more challenging for them, it is still great fun. Brightly colored cones marked the area around the equipment and formed a make-shift route ending with an elevated pause table. Reaching and sitting on that table marks the end of the course for each participant.

OMG! I had an agility course in my very own yard! How did my mom know that agility was my third option as a potential career? Just when I thought that she had done nearly everything that was kind and good for me, she went a step further and made my dream come true in my very own yard.

That beats getting the marrow in the dog bone any day! My mom was the best!

As it turned out, the agility course was just the beginning of her planned good time for me. As I heard the back gate open, Cousin Carolyn walked in with her dog

named Riggins. When I first met Cousin Carolyn a few months ago, she told me that she wanted me to meet Riggins someday. Well, today was that special day. Riggins, a very handsome Golden Retriever, approached me in a most polite manner. He was not just a Dog's Dog like Finnegan, but an Elite Dog's Dog! I was immediately love-struck not just by his good looks, but, more importantly, by the kindness reflected in his eyes. That

Riggins was awesome.

sparkle in his eyes revealed that he was just as smitten with me. We just stared at each other for a while, gave appropriate sniffs, play bowed to each other and then went off to play with Kessen and Brightie.

After Kessen, Brightie, Riggins and I did the ritualistic sniff and bow routine to each other, we enthusiastically ran around the yard checking out

We were meant for each other.

all of the various forms of equipment. The excitement level

was intense for all of us and was comparable to being thrust into a huge treat bowl filled with goodies. In the history of play dates, this had to be the best one ever planned and put into action!

Just love playing in the yard.

Just when I needed a pick-me-up the most, my mom planned this utterly, incredible play date. I did, indeed, have another athletic option for championship glory, and my weight wouldn't get in the way of this one. Speed, accuracy and attention to a handler's direction were all I needed for success. I definitely had speed, was fairly precise in terms of details and even learned to pay attention. Due to my assistance training, I had better impulse control than I had a few months ago, so the agility option had possibilities. Thinking ahead, the only problem was convincing my mom to be my handler, and once again, the language barrier got in the way of progress.

I really needed to stop this thought process and get a paw-hold on reality. Today was meant for fun with Kessen, Brightie and my new friend, Riggins...not for getting my mom to be my handler. That was a project for another day. Running, jumping and goofing around with the equipment was the object of this play date, and I was going to take full advantage of it with the group. Let the games begin!

Because Riggins was our guest, we wanted him to go first, but he declined. Apparently, he wanted to see just what was expected of him before he ventured onto this make-shift course filled with unusual obstacles. Wanting to show Riggins that I was not only gorgeous but spirited, I marched onto the course looking like I knew what I was doing. I favored the seesaw because it looked challenging and didn't require any jumping. It had a plank that went up to a peak and down as the dog moved towards the bottom. There was a large pad under the base of the plank that would absorb the shock of the board hitting the ground as the dog moved downward toward the opposite end of the seesaw.

Months ago at the dog festival, I saw the dogs go up and down the seesaw with relative ease during the agility demonstration, and it didn't look very difficult to me at the time. Sure, it took balance and precision, but I was convinced that I had those skills. I was pretty agile and not unusually clumsy, so going up and down this seesaw was going to be both fun and relatively easy.

Once again, I was incorrect in my assessment of my capabilities. On my very first attempt at the seesaw, I never made it past the half-way mark of the incline before I quickly lost my balance and toppled off. Kessen, Brightie and Riggins were watching from the sidelines and hooted loudly at my awkward dismount. (*I think they were taking bets against my making it!*) For my next attempt, I approached the seesaw at a slower pace and carefully walked the length of the plank going up, but then suddenly realized that what goes up must basically come down. I wasn't prepared for that descending sensation…not by a long shot. Upon losing my balance on the downward slope, my jump from the seesaw was quite the sight. This challenge was definitely much harder than I thought, but I was not giving up. On my third attempt, I managed to make it up and down without falling off the plank. However, on the

It's not as easy as it looks!

way down, I ended up straddling a portion of the seesaw but recovered quickly. It wasn't a pretty sight by any stretch of the imagination. Upon successfully reaching the bottom and thankfully being splinter-free, I turned and bowed to my skeptical audience. They all howled their approval for my completion of the task but gave very few points for my technique. Spectators are often such harsh critics!

Riggins took the next turn at the equipment, and he preferred the single, double and triple jumps. Looking over the equipment before making any attempt gave him a sense of how much speed he needed to complete the three jumps. (*Why didn't I think of that before making a complete fool of myself on the seesaw?*) Gathering momentum, Riggins effortlessly sailed over each of the three jumps as if he had wings. What an amazing display of speed and athletic skill. Our having paws prevented us from applauding, but we howled enthusiastically following his final jump. He was quite the athlete!

Brightie is an agility queen.

Brightie was next, and she favored the tunnel since she could run in and out at great speeds. We watched her body bounding effortlessly through the tunnel's inner fabric as she raced through the length of it. She was a natural tunnel babe! Once out the other end, she reversed her strategy, ran back through it the other way and gave a flamboyant bow after exiting the tunnel. What a show off!

The elevated pause table was Kessen's preferred choice because all he had to do was position himself comfortably on it. He left our group and sauntered up to the pause table. Turning to us, he bowed as only a king holding court would do and jumped onto the pause table. From there, he watched the activities from a heightened vantage point without ever moving a muscle. That was definitely Kessen's favorite form of exercise!

Riggins, Brightie and I then ran around the other forms of equipment, attempting each one, knocking over various cones and just having a good time. At one point, Brightie grabbed one of the colorful cones and raced around with that cone in her mouth. She was definitely having a great time, but carrying that cone in her mouth made her look like she was wearing a dunce cap! In the meantime, Riggins sailed back and forth through the tire jump while I raced in and out of the tunnel. Going through the weave poles was confusing, but we

This is so refreshing.

still had fun while bumping into each other. By the time we tried all of the equipment, we were exhausted and headed for the shade of the maple tree and the cool water in the pool. While we dunked our paws in the water, Kessen decided to leave his elevated position on the pause table and joined us in the shade. However, he never got close to the baby pool that he once thought was an oversized water bowl!

While we rested, the folks and Cousin Carolyn talked about how much fun we had with the make-shift agility course. Riggins was my new, special friend. Thanks to my mom's great play date, I was no longer wallowing in self-pity. Her plan really worked. Then, the unexpected happened. The folks and Cousin Carolyn had leashes in their hands and were going to be our handlers for the course. They watched us running around the various forms of obstacles on the course and decided that they would participate in the fun as well. We were going to have a make-believe agility competition.

OMG! Does it get any better than this? Kessen, seeing the prospect of likely participation in further exertion of energy, resumed his relaxed position on the pause table. He was having absolutely nothing to do with this. Brightie, Riggins and I couldn't wait for the opportunity to show how versatile we were on the equipment. This time, Riggins and Cousin Carolyn went first, and she guided him through the course as if she had done this before. Riggins followed her direction with the best eye contact I had ever seen. He wasn't just a good looking, athletic dog. My instincts told me that Riggins was definitely a ringer in terms of agility! The rest of us didn't stand a chance.

Brightie was the next competitor with my dad guiding her through the course. She pranced her way around the course looking like a graceful ballerina and needed very little direction. She had a distinct familiarity with the course which led me to believe that she had done this before. Ending with a leap onto the pause table, Brightie actually forced Kessen to exert some energy in order to move out of her way.

I was the last competitor and knew this was my moment to impress Riggins. With my mom as my handler, we approached each obstacle with precision and intensity. I went over the jumps that fortunately weren't very high and slowly walked up and down the dreaded seesaw as carefully as I could. Since straddling the equipment wasn't appropriate, I recognized that being splinter free was essential for my image as a champion athlete and future girlfriend of Riggins. Flying effortlessly through the tire jump gave me the confidence to race through the tunnel at top speed. After coming out the other end of the tunnel, all I had to face were the dreaded weave poles. Unfortunately, I got tangled in them. Weaving in and out was a bit confusing, but that's what made the course challenging. While it wasn't my best performance, I raced to the pause table and confidently took my place next to Kessen, Riggins and Brightie. We were all winners, and it sure felt great. I was pretty good at this and with hard work and perseverance, a career in competitive agility just might be a possibility for me. At least, it was an option, and that was all that mattered.

As our play date came to an end, I was sad to see Riggins leave, but I knew we'd see each other again. After all, we were destined for a future together, and nothing gets in the way of destiny. Realizing that I had other career choices was an added bonus on this day of fun and special games. However, at

Riggins had to leave.

this moment in time, I just enjoyed the fact that my life was full of sunshine again because of family, friends and renewed confidence in myself. I was definitely moving on...

21

Back In Time

The day after that outstanding play date, Kessen, Brightie and I still reeled from the excitement as well as the exhaustion from the agility equipment. Even though it wasn't a regulation course by any stretch of the imagination, that agility equipment forced us to use muscles that we never knew we had. As tired as we were, we would do it all over again if we had the opportunity. At least, Brightie and I would. Kessen would probably make his way to the pause table and call it an "exhausting job well done!"

Because Brightie was so adept at negotiating the equipment, I actually thought she had done agility work before our play date. With little direction from our dad, she seemed to know exactly where she was going on the course and what to do with each form of equipment as she approached it. I told her how very impressed I was with her skillful exhibition. Imagine my surprise when she fluttered those long, curly eyelashes at me and confessed that both she and Kessen had taken an agility class a few years ago.

I asked them why they never told me about their agility experience, and Kessen reluctantly explained their silence. Since my dreams of athletic success meant so much to me, they didn't want me to feel short-changed because I wasn't given the same opportunities they were. They knew I had some setbacks with the dock diving and the disc dog fiasco, so they thought it best to say nothing about their agility experiences.

That was so very kind of them to shield me from any additional sadness. After all, I had to give up on the dock diving and the disc dog career for various reasons. Having now had the agility experience, I knew it was a clear-cut possibility for me. My fear of deep water or my weight would not get in my way of future success. All I had to do was overcome the language barrier with my mom, but that was easier said than done. For now, I wasn't going to think about that. Instead, I really wanted to hear all about their agility training from beginning to end.

Going back in time, Kessen's version began with Brightie's surprising ability with the class. Working with our mom as her handler, Brightie had a natural talent for following our mom's directions and had the speed to negotiate the equipment with little difficulty. According to Kessen's recollection, Brightie worked off-leash which gave her an advantage since she wasn't dragging anything behind her while completing the course. Her aptitude for agility work coupled with her natural speed made her quite a contender in the class. The beginners in the class admired her talent while the advanced dogs recognized a new threat to their competition status. Brightie, on the other paw, said that she was just there to have fun and that she did.

Sailing through the course at great speed, Brightie's scores put her in the second place position in the class competition. Kessen actually thought she earned first place

Don't you think a recount is a reasonable request?

and demanded a recount of the timing, but no one listened to him. Because she maneuvered the course with such ease, Brightie didn't feel that she really worked hard enough for first place. The ultimate winner of the competition had trained for weeks for that event. All Brightie did was show up and run the course, so second place was fine with her. She really didn't need a first place ribbon to know that she was successful. I wished that I had her confidence!

Brightie's version of Kessen's performance in the agility competition was quite the opposite. With our dad as his handler, Kessen often strayed off the course to introduce himself to a new dog in the class or investigate a new scent buried behind a barrier of some sort. (*Our stately leader of the pack did that?*) According to Brightie, Kessen was such a comedian that he cared very little about winning. Because of that, he lacked the focus necessary for agility competition. The folks wanted both dogs to have fun in the class, but Kessen's idea of fun was clowning around with the equipment and using the class for networking with new classmates. Consequently, he was kept on a long leash while going through the course. That alone slowed his ability to negotiate the obstacles quickly, but Kessen didn't mind. His reputation as class clown followed him throughout the duration of the classes. Brightie also said that most of the classmates enjoyed his antics. The diehard competitors were quite distracted and not at all happy. Once again, Kessen didn't care about their disapproval. He had his following of adoring fans, and that's all that mattered to him. Even back then, he was a leader of sorts!

Now came the best part of Brightie's story. The last class of the session was an actual competition in terms of scoring points and timing. The energy levels were high in the room, and excitement filled the air. Rather than focus on the course, Kessen schmoozed with a gorgeous West Highland Terrier on the sidelines. Dad was getting nervous because all of the dogs were going to be off-leash during the competition, and he knew how unreliable Kessen was off-leash. As a result, he clutched bits of dried liver and cheese in his hand to use as lures in case Kessen decided to stray from the course.

Mom and Brightie watched the Dad-Kessen Team from the sidelines and anxiously awaited their completion of the course. According to Brightie, Kessen's experience was almost flawless, but "almost" was the key word. He was actually taking this competition seriously, and that fact alone took the audience by surprise...until he got to the seesaw. Kessen went up and down with ease and was on his way to the pause table when he stopped in his tracks. He turned and spotted the folded towel that had been placed under the board of the seesaw. That towel was meant to absorb the shock of the dog's weight when coming down the other side of the seesaw. In that decision-making moment, Kessen chose clowning around to winning. He ran to that seesaw, grabbed the towel and proceeded to run around the room with that towel flying high as his victory flag. Dogs barked, handlers attempted to calm their dogs, our folks were embarrassed and Brightie howled with delight. Mom finally went onto the course with hands on hips which signaled the end of Kessen's victory laps. Once his leash was attached, Kessen was led off the course. Brightie remembered that in spite of his eventual consequences for this behavior, Kessen actually winked at that West Highland Terrier on his way out. They all just left the training facility in silence. Needless to say, they never took Kessen there again. To this day, Brightie laughs every time she thinks about the situation. Kessen, on the other paw, never mentions it at all.

Throughout the day, I thought about Kessen and Brightie's experiences in their agility class and laughed each time I thought about them. Knowing full well that they

When you've got it, flaunt it!

experienced something I truly wanted to do by no means saddened me. Instead, I was grateful that they shared those memories with me, and each time I replayed them in my mind, they made me smile from ear to ear. They were truly fun friends!

Sometimes when no options seem forthcoming, an event happens that changes everything. While resting in my kennel, I heard the folks talking about the agility play date and how much I enjoyed it. Since I only had two more months before I went off to Advanced Training, they actually enrolled me in an agility class as their final gift to me. Once again...OMG! My dream was coming true, and I didn't even have to deal with the language barrier. That news launched me over the proverbial doghouse with happiness, and I couldn't wait to get started with the class...

22

Easy Does It

The following week was the launch of what might be my future career…the agility class. My excitement level was so high that I only had time to nod to Kessen and Brightie as I left the house with the folks. The class happened to be in the same training facility that Kessen and Brightie attended a few years ago. Hopefully, they didn't remember his youthful foolishness.

The car ride seemed endless when it was actually only twenty minutes of driving time. Nevertheless, I had difficulty following my proper automobile exit protocols, but I somehow managed to carry them off. I had to keep reminding myself that "easy does it" gets me to where I want to go since rushing into things just takes longer to get there. Hearing the sounds of dogs

My dream is coming true.

barking just heightened my excitement. Nevertheless, I managed to enter the facility without excessive pulling or lunging because those behaviors only made actually getting into a room take longer than necessary. Since my mom's words "rise to the occasion" regarding her expectations of me echoed in my head, I was on my best behavior for this event.

As we entered, I stopped and stared at what might be my dream come true. Right in front of me was an official, regulation agility course. All the equipment a dog might imagine was staring me in the eyes, and I just couldn't wait to get started and live my dream.

There were only two other dogs in the class...a black and white, energetic Border Collie named Jax and a rust and white, multi-colored Jack Russell Terrier named Flip. I was the largest dog in the class, but that fact didn't bother me at all. The handlers listened intently as the instructor introduced herself and discussed the safe usage of each form of equipment. Judging from her tone of voice, this instructor had no time for nonsense. Luckily, Kessen wasn't with us!

Since we, as dogs, really didn't understand what was being said, the three of us shared information with each other in our own way. Flip and Jax had already completed an agility class at another facility and were using this one as a means of gaining more speed and familiarity with the equipment. Their having prior experience with a course didn't faze me because, in many respects, I had been preparing for this class for the last thirteen months. My jumping, twirling, spinning and running in the house and in the yard prepared me for some form of athletic competition. Agility fit right into my training program which was meant to develop well-toned muscles and increased stamina. Since pivoting quickly around the course was essential, even repeatedly getting the *zooms* served their purpose. All of my hard work prepared me for this, and my competence on the make-shift agility course in my yard only proved that fact. I had nothing to worry about with these two competitors. Even though I was the largest dog in the class, my confidence matched my size! Their having past experience wasn't a threat to me.

While we were waiting for the class to actually start, Flip, the Jack Russell Terrier, asked if either of us heard the legend of the mysterious dog whose spirit haunted the equipment of this particular agility course? Jax and I looked at each other and didn't know if we should laugh or not. According to Flip, a dog from the previous class told her a scary legend that concerned this training facility and especially the agility course. According to the legend, this infamous dog had the competition win in the proverbial dog bowl, but forfeited it by running around the course while using the towel from under the seesaw as his victory flag. His clowning around to amuse the audience cost him the victory, and his not taking the course seriously angered the agility gods. As a consequence for his disrespect, the dog's spirit was not allowed to move on from this facility. To this day, it haunted the course as dogs traversed the equipment.

According to the story told to Flip, dogs have reported hearing chilling, howling sounds when going through the darkened closed tunnel. That tunnel had its exit covered, and dogs blindly negotiated the tunnel in order to reach the way out. Since the closed tunnel was dark, dogs reported even seeing the spirit's face against the fabric of the tunnel. As a result, dogs often panicked in the closed tunnel. There was no other reason for that reaction other than the presence of the spirit.

Jax, the Border Collie, listened intently while looking for some indication of a ruse on Flip's face during the telling of this legend. Perhaps Flip attempted to frighten us with this tale in order to gain an advantage over us on the course. But, Flip looked pretty serious about what she was told by the other dog and looked apprehensively at the dreaded closed tunnel. I, on the other paw, knew immediately that Flip was talking about Kessen's display of clown-like behavior during the agility competition years ago. However, I wasn't going to say anything to refute the legend. I thought it was cool that Kessen was now a legendary figure in this facility and couldn't wait to tell him about his status when I got home. For now, I just kept it to myself... especially the part about the closed tunnel. After all, I personally knew and lived with the legendary spirit!

The class began, and we familiarized ourselves with the various forms of equipment. I laughed to myself when both Jax and Flip balked at the closed tunnel. That legendary spirit was definitely working for me in this class. I flew through that closed tunnel with ease, and both dogs were amazed at my courage. I told them to face their fears and not let fear stop them from being successful. (*I should be ashamed of myself, but I wasn't!*) I was just having fun with them. Besides, when they finally go through that closed tunnel, they'll be stronger for doing it. In a vague sense, I was just lending a paw to building confidence and character in the face of adversity. (*It's official...I'm shameless!*)

That first agility class was so much fun, and I was anxious to complete all of the sessions. Jax, Flip and I were becoming friendly competitors and cheered each other on while going through the course. I told them all about my dreams of athletic glory, and how my long-standing desire to be a champion was clouded by my recent enjoyment of assistance work. They didn't have any dreams like mine. They just wanted to demonstrate some skill in agility and perhaps go on to further competitions. I was the only one who faced these career-changing decisions.

I never mentioned the spirit legend to them again, but chuckled to myself every time I approached that closed tunnel. Maybe I'd see Kessen's face one day or hear his howling echoing through the tunnel's fabric. If that ever happened, he'd have the last laugh for sure because that would surely make me run even faster. I'd look like I was shot out of a cannon from that tunnel.

My dream came true with this agility class, and even if they were competitors, I had two new friends to share it with me. Being so impulsive, I had to keep reminding myself that "easy does it" made things happen. I was in the class for the fun and not for the difficult career choices that weighed heavily on my mind for months. Enjoyment of the class and bonding with my new friends were my priorities. During the next few weeks, I'd remind myself that "easy does it" gets me where I want to go...

23

Load Up On Fun

The weeks were flying by as my time here at the sorority house was coming to an end. In a few weeks, I was scheduled to enter into Advanced Training or Puppy College as it is called. That is the most rigorous part of assistance dog training, and only the best prepared and qualified dogs succeed. I had to make some major career decisions soon, or regrets would take over my life.

The agility class was such a successful venture for me, and according to the instructor, I demonstrated great promise in that area. The seesaw was no longer a threat to my balance and was now a splinter free form of equipment. Everything in terms of the class fell into place due to my earlier running, twirling and pivoting exercises. Contrary to popular human belief, *zooming* had a purpose, and my pivoting expertise attested to that fact. There definitely was championship potential in my future.

Flip and Jax did well in the class and no longer feared the dreaded, closed tunnel on the course. In fact, they participated in a few competitions prior to this class and even won ribbons. Their future was definitely within the competitive realm, but was that meant for me as well?

While I was excited about the possibility of a career in competitive agility, I experienced some minor reservations regarding that choice. How that happened, I'll never know. All I could think about for the last fourteen months was an athletic career with me destined for championship glory, trophies and ribbons. Now, I had these nagging regrets about leaving my assistance training behind for athletic endeavors. Somehow choosing agility over assistance seemed superficial and not at all as rewarding as helping others. That thought seemed totally contradictory to my earlier beliefs.

As early as my puppy days with my siblings, I wanted a career in some form of athletic venture. As it turned out, competitive agility was the appropriate decision for me, and I was unquestionably good at it. My talent, strength and stamina were proof of potential success in that career choice. Why was I having regrets about pursuing it and leaving an assistance career behind? Having to choose between assistance and agility constantly bounced around my mind. I had to find some way to ease this confusion, and to do that, I had to examine my feelings regarding past experiences. (*There's that touchy-feely stuff again!*)

During the last few months I made major changes in my home and public behavior. *Zooming* in the house was a thing of the past, and I couldn't even remember the last time I refused to leave a public place. I no longer resisted getting out of the car and hadn't hugged the street while refusing to walk properly in ages. I looked forward to wearing my cape and even felt a degree of pride when I wore it. Deon's words of wisdom came to mind when he told me that his cape was his trophy, and it meant more than ribbons and awards. Now, I know what he meant by that since I felt the same way when I wore mine. He also said that when dreams come true, there is sometimes an element of regret. At the time, I thought our conversation was such a downer and never believed that feeling would ever occur. Nevertheless, I was faced with regrets when my dream of athletic fame was within my grasp.

Having to choose between the two was just too difficult. On one paw, I thoroughly enjoyed the excitement of competitive agility; on the other paw, I had recently discovered a respect and love for possibly helping others through a career in assistance. To my surprise, trophies and ribbons never entered into my current thought process. I actually didn't need them anymore to feel successful. (*What was happening to me?*)

Kessen and Brightie had their own views on the subject. While Brightie was genuinely supportive of an assistance career for me, she couldn't believe that I'd even consider giving up the opportunity for ribbons and awards that she hoped would decorate my kennel walls. Not having them would thoroughly alter the canine feng shui that she had planned for my area.

Decorating inspires inner peace.

Kessen, on the other paw, would not give an opinion one way or the other. Months ago when I told Kessen that career decisions were mine to make, I didn't realize that one day I'd be asking his advice on the matter. Kessen left that decision entirely up to me but added that I needed to do what made me happy and not what others told me to do. Kessen was truly a wise leader of the pack.

Even though I was preoccupied with this dilemma, I was making the rounds of some of the public places with the folks today. When I saw my cape and leash in my mom's hands, I ran to the back door and assumed a perfect sitting position. I really enjoy going out and can't believe that I was such a brat in my earlier months. In hindsight, all of those ridiculous refusals were merely puppy behaviors and not something suitable for an adult dog. After all, I was over a year old now and had to act my age...especially while in public and wearing my cape.

Our first stop was the neighborhood coffee shop, and I realized that I didn't even care that I was positioned under the table. I didn't think of that location as the cheap seats anymore. People stopped to greet me and even praised my behavior. That was almost like getting a blue ribbon or at least close to winning one.

Months ago, the folks had promised to take me to a huge indoor mall when my behavior improved, and today was the day. At first, walking into this gigantic place was a bit intimidating, but I gradually got used to the shiny floors and the reflection of the lights from the high ceilings. Off in the distance, I heard what sounded like a train whistle, but what would a train be doing indoors? My folks moved me off to the side and out of the way of a moving train. It wasn't the typical train one might see at a station but a kiddies' train with children occupying the seats. They actually waved to me as the train went by. While I wished that I could have waved back, my paws just don't move that way. Instead, I gave them my best smile and special helicopter wag of the tail as they went by. I watched the train disappear in the distance and hoped that it would come back this way again.

As I became accustomed to the shiny floors that tended to be a bit slippery, we arrived at the center of the mall that had numerous restaurants, seating and an area that had something called Dancing Waters. I never heard of anything like that before. I had seen Brightie make bubbles in her water bowl, but I didn't think that was going to happen here. The folks sat on a bench and positioned me next to them. While I didn't know what we were waiting for, it had to be something special. All of a sudden, exhilarating music filled the area. Surprise of all surprises, water began spouting out of holes in the floor. Flowing at various heights in different areas, the water seemed to be dancing to the music. It was such an incredible sight since I never knew water could do that. When the song ended, the water gently returned to the holes in the floor. This was such an amazing sight to see, and I couldn't wait to tell Kessen and Brightie all about it. My folks were working towards a gold medal with this outing, and I was definitely loading up on fun.

This mall was like an amusement park; and to my surprise, it even had a ride. We approached a box-like structure with glass doors on all sides and a door that slid open. Since it went up and down to various levels of the mall with people riding inside, I just guessed that it was some sort of ride. I watched it go up a few levels, stop and let people off. Then, people got in and rode down to the main floor. When it reached the bottom level, we allowed the people to exit and waited our turn to enter.

I have to admit that I was a bit nervous at first since I had never been in anything like this before. After all, it went pretty high into the air, and I didn't know if the height would frighten me. However, I was about to find out. As the doors slid closed, I positioned myself by one of the glass sides and braced myself for the upward motion. The feeling was a bit unnerving, but my mom gave me a few treats on the way up. To be honest, I had to use my sense of smell for the treats since I had my eyes closed all the way up. The doors opened, but we didn't exit the ride. We were now going to go down and back to where we started. The feeling going down wasn't as scary as going up, but I still had my eyes closed. When we got to the bottom, the folks asked if I wanted to try it again. I was impressed that they wanted my opinion, but the only way I could show my enthusiasm was to wag my tail. To my astonishment, they took that as a *yes*. (*Was I now learning to communicate with them?*) So once again, we went up and down, but this time, I had my eyes open. It wasn't scary anymore, and I happily grabbed those treats put in front of me. After getting out of the ride, we walked around the mall for a while and then went on that ride again. I wasn't fearful at all and was amazed at all the sights to be seen from such a lofty position. This outing was just the best ever!

When we got back to the house, I raced to tell Kessen and Brightie about my mall experience. I told them every detail that I could remember from walking into the place, the shiny floors, the lights, the shops, the people, the Dancing Waters and the numerous rides up and down in the glass box. Brightie wanted to know all there was to tell about the Dancing Waters. She listened intently to my description of the experience. I wished that she could have experienced it with me. Later that evening, I saw Brightie attempting to hum while making bubbles in her water bowl. It certainly wasn't the same as the Dancing Waters, but it sure made me laugh!

Kessen listened to the details of my excursion and smiled a bit when I talked about riding up and down in the glass box. I told him how scary it was at first, but how I got used to going up and down after a few rides. I didn't know the name of the ride, but Kessen seemed to know. (*He knew everything!*) Kessen said that it was, indeed, a ride, but not intended for fun. It was meant to carry people to different levels so they wouldn't have to use the stairs, and that glass box was called an elevator. In spite of Kessen's explanation, I still considered it a ride, but now it had a name...the Glass Box Elevator.

I really loaded up on fun at the mall and would remember it for a long time. Surprisingly, I didn't give any thought to my career dilemma, and what a relief that was. Tomorrow, I'd go to my agility class, and I couldn't wait to tell Jax and Flip about my excursion to the mall and my rides in the glass box. They would enjoy hearing about that. We only had two more classes before the session ended, and that timeline signaled my decision-making deadline once and for all. Maybe Jax or Flip would have some suggestions regarding career choices. I'd be sure to ask them tomorrow.

After a restless night, I wasn't at my best for agility competition, but my energy resurfaced when I saw Jax and Flip in the facility. They were all excited about the upcoming competition that was to take place on the last day of class. It was supposedly a big event, and lots of people attended with their dogs. Most were agility competitors who wanted to see what competition was out there for future events. The winner of this event would undoubtedly be a threat to their dog's chances of winning in the future. This was a championship event... complete with trophies and ribbons.

While our handlers walked the course prior to our running it, I told Jax and Flip about my excursion to the mall. They thoroughly enjoyed every detail...especially about the rides in the Glass Box Elevator. They had never been on anything like that and considered me quite brave to have done it more than once. They believed me to be quite fearless since I was never even frightened by the prospect of a "spirit" in the closed tunnel. (*I really should tell them, but I won't!*)

One by one, we went through a practice run on the course. We were all a bit off on that first run. Because I was distracted by the thoughts racing through my mind, my timing wasn't very good. Jax tapped a few jumps by not reaching the proper elevation, and Flip lost her balance on the seesaw. We were all a mess and made mistakes that we never made before. It must be due to the stress of the upcoming competition, but we had to put that aside for now and concentrate on the course.

During the next attempt, Jax regained his concentration and had a successful run through the course. Flip went a bit slower on the seesaw in an effort to keep her balance. Nevertheless, she made up for her time by bolting through the closed tunnel. The possibility of hearing or seeing the "spirit" didn't slow her down at all. I attempted to outrun my thoughts by flying over, under, in and through the various forms of equipment at top speed. Those maneuvers gave me my fastest time ever on the course. Judging from the results, we were all back in sync and prepared for the championship competition next week.

While we rested, I told Jax and Flip about my career dilemma and how it seemed to be a no-win situation. While I enjoyed agility, I also had this newfound respect and admiration for assistance work. Because assistance work filled me with pride and gave me a sense of being useful to others, I seemed to be leaning toward that career. Yet, my entire life from early puppy days to the present was geared toward athletic achievement. I had to give up something, but what was the right thing to do? What career road was the right one for me?

Flip sighed at the seriousness of my dilemma and wasn't sure how to advise me. She knew that I was not only good at agility but was also one of her fierce competitors. Flip also saw the delight in my face when I told her about my mall experience and the thrill involved in my public outings. Her only advice was to do what I thought was best for me and not what others expect me to do. It was advice that I had heard before, but it was easier said than done.

Jax, on the other paw, recognized the importance of my dilemma as well, but proposed a practical yet simple solution to the problem. Since the final competition was next week, why not let the outcome of the competition determine my choice? If I were skilled enough to win against the two of them, competitive agility was the way to go in terms of a career. After all, they were seasoned competitors and were going to be tough to beat. Only a talented competitor would accomplish that, and if I did, I'd be a top contender for future championships. Having that talent and potential were appropriate reasons to continue with agility.

Jax's solution was interesting, but it didn't take into account my feelings. (*Once again, those pesky feelings intrude!*) I definitely had the skill and determination to win that competition, but would winning make my decision even more difficult? Nevertheless, I decided right then and there that I would take that chance. Maybe at some point during the competition, I'd come to a decision on my own. If not, the outcome of the competition would determine my future career.

This next week would give me time to think about everything. I believed that not only would I win, but I would also make the right choice in the end. That would be a defining moment for me and for my future. I only hoped that once a decision was made, I'd be prepared for the outcome...

I have some thinking to do.

24

Off To The Races

During the week before the big day, I was busier than ever. My days were spent perfecting my assistance commands and visiting a variety of public places such as libraries, restaurants, offices and malls. Attending a church service rounded out the week, and it was an appropriate way to prepare my mind for the big event. In the past, church services were calming events, so this particular one was important to my peace of mind.

Keeping fit is essential.

Working on my physical shape was essential as well. The early evenings were spent exercising in the yard while Kessen and Brightie offered tips for improving various jumping and pivoting maneuvers. Sammy watched from the other side of the fence but never offered any suggestions for improvement on my part. He never offered advice without being asked for his opinion, and that fact alone made him such a classy dog! Finnegan, on the other paw, raced around the perimeter of the property a few times and offered tips on how to win over the judges during the competition. According to him, it was all about finesse…having it and using it when it counted. His approach to life was unique and ever so fascinating!

Cousin Carolyn brought Riggins for another play date, and we spent the afternoon playing on make-believe agility equipment. We jumped over imaginary hurdles and ran in between the bushes pretending they were the weave poles. Fortunately, the folks owned the tunnel used in the first agility play date and kept it positioned in the yard for our use. Having an actual tunnel to challenge us was such fun, and we took turns running back and forth through it.

After gnawing on a twig, Brightie joined in and really showed us how a true agility aficionado completed an imaginary course. Seeing her run, jump, pivot and weave through a make-believe course was like watching a graceful ballerina during a performance. Riggins and I were so impressed with her imaginary course that we joined in for more fun and games. Kessen observed our antics for a while from his stationary position under the shade of the maple tree before falling sound asleep in the grass. I guess watching us play was exhausting!

Riggins and I spent a lot of time together, and he was quite supportive regarding my upcoming competition. His only words of advice were to clear my mind of all negative thoughts, follow the course, do my best and imagine myself as the winner. After all, winning was my dream since I was a puppy, and dreams often come true. He was such a good friend to offer such wise advice. Riggins and Cousin Carolyn left that afternoon, and I immediately missed him. His support meant so much to me, and I'd remember his incredible words of guidance throughout the competition.

Riggins had the best advice.

After months and months of training, that extra special day of reckoning was almost here. Anticipation, excitement as well as anxiety filled my senses as the day approached. While my days were filled with numerous activities that kept me alert, my nights were restless due to endless energetic thoughts racing through my mind. The night before the big event, I just couldn't fall asleep. I was tossing and turning in my kennel when Kessen stopped by for a brief Kennel Korner chat and gave me a special, little relaxation tip to use during competition. He encouraged me to look into the audience for friendly faces. According to him, seeing

Look to your friends for support.

family members and good friends cheering you on was a great confidence booster. That seemed like very good advice, and I was happy that he stopped by. Just when I thought he was leaving, Kessen turned around, looked deeply into my eyes and reminded me that all I had to do was follow my heart, and the rest would fall into place. His sincere concern and reassurance allowed me to fall into a deep sleep…deeper than I had slept in weeks.

Morning came, and I felt refreshed for the first time in days. It was the day of the big event. While the folks prepared my traveling bag, I attempted to breathe normally in spite of my heightened apprehension. Watching them fill that bag with treats, water bowl, paper towels, a water bottle and

You can do this!

cooling collar heightened my anxiety. Finally, my traveling bag was fully loaded. As the entire family headed for the back door, I thought of Kessen's soothing words of wisdom from the night before. That advice allowed me to get a good night's rest for the first time this past week and continued to calm my nerves a bit before we left. I knew that I was physically prepared and capable of winning this competition, but following my heart would undoubtedly help me make the best decision in terms of my future. After all, Kessen was the pack leader and could always be trusted to give good advice. With those thoughts echoing in my mind, we left the house and were off to the races!

Entering the facility, I was taken aback by the crowds of spectators and their dogs in the seating area. While their numerous conversations created tremendous background noise, their barking and howling dogs added to the intense level of excitement in the air. All of the sounds seemed to blend into one, giant distraction. While I attempted to block it all out, I wasn't successful at all.

The area looked so much larger with the additional seating and looked more like an arena than the usual training area. Taking Kessen's advice, I scanned the crowd and caught a glimpse of my family members seated in the audience. Seeing their happy faces had such a relaxing effect on me. Kessen was right once again. Dad, Kessen and Brightie sat next to Auntie Carol and Auntie Fran in one row. Strangely, when I saw Auntie Fran, I got that special *tingle* again that reminded me of my birth mother's love. That singular sensation reassured me that my birth mother was also with me on today's journey and that boosted my confidence. In the next row, I saw my Cousin Steven, Cousin Carolyn and my very good friend Riggins all smiling when they saw me. Cousin Steven gave me the "thumbs up" signal for encouragement. Riggins would have done the same, but dogs don't have thumbs. Even if they did, paws just don't work that way. Instead, Riggins gave a special wink and smile of approval. That was more than enough support for me.

While anxiously scanning the crowd, I caught a glimpse of Deon, the first service dog I had ever met. What was he doing here? He still looked as regal as ever while sitting with his partner. As I recall, he not only listened to my cluttered thoughts about championship glory but also gave me some sound words of wisdom that shaped my future actions. Because of Deon, I

You go girl!

stopped running from my cape and learned to value wearing it as a type of trophy for good works... just as he valued his. I'm so very grateful for his contribution to my well-being. Seeing him out there today supporting my efforts was such a confidence builder. What a great dog!

Not far from Deon was another stunning service dog who looked quite familiar. Taking a closer look, I recognized her...it was Kelyna, the Golden Retriever who was the service dog for a hearing impaired individual. I remembered that she was trained by my folk's friend Jan, a certified dog trainer, in North Carolina. While in training for assistance, Kelyna was torn between a career in canine freestyle dancing and that of

assistance. While she really loved losing herself in the dancing to the music, she gave up a possible profession in the theater for a career in assistance. According to Kelyna, it really wasn't a difficult decision to choose helping people above dancing in the theater.

She loves helping others.

At a time when decisions seemed impossible for me, her apparent dedication was a real inspiration. When we met months ago, she was quite concerned about my future career decisions, but she was here today supporting me. Having her here today to support my efforts meant so much to me. I regarded Kelyna as a significant role model, and her being here was proof that canine camaraderie was an amazing bond shared by dogs.

Just when things couldn't get any better, I spotted Carlita in the crowd. Being the most gorgeous English Golden Retriever, she sat confidently with her partner who was a returning veteran. As a service dog, her job took precedence over everything. Carlita never got carried away with the unusual attention showered upon her due to her stunning appearance. She either didn't realize that she was gorgeous, or she didn't care about it. Service was her calling, and nothing got in the way of that. Yet, here

Follow your dream!

she was today supporting my efforts. I wish that I could run up to her and thank her, but that wasn't possible. Instead, I just nodded to her in appreciation of her being here today, and she nodded back in approval.

Jax and Flip were waiting for me near the starting line with their handlers, and they seemed as anxious as I was while waiting for the event to begin. As I glanced around the arena, the significance of this event seemed to overwhelm me.

This was, indeed, my moment of truth…I took my place with my mom beside them and waited for the event to start.

Before the event began, the handlers were given an opportunity to walk the course so they'd know how to direct us through the equipment when the competition began. My mom reassured me that she knew what she was doing, and all was well as long as I followed her cues. After the opening ceremonies (*This was really a big event!*), the first contestant was called. Through a process I didn't understand, I was the first to run through the course. Since my mom had already walked the course, I knew that all I had to do was follow her direction in order to have a decent score. While I can't remember any of it due to an onset of nervous energy, I ended up with a great first score in both time and points. I'll never know how I managed to accomplish that!

Once I regained partial control of my senses, I followed my mom's cues on my second run. Much to my surprise, the scores were even higher than the first attempt. Sitting on that pause table and realizing that I had done everything I could to win this event was so exhilarating. Nevertheless, the actual running of the course in each attempt was a total blur in my mind. Had my anxiety shielded me from the actual competition? All of my preparation for the last fifteen months was working for me in terms of success, but that trophy wasn't mine yet. Jax and Flip still had to compete against my highest time and total points in order to take over first place.

Since my part in the competition was over, Jax and Flip had to compete against each other for higher scores in order to beat mine. During their first runs, each competitor experienced some difficulties in terms of distractions causing some loss of points. Jax had an issue with a Miniature Poodle who was sitting on the sidelines and momentarily stole his attention, while Flip was distracted by a handful of multi-colored balloons flapping in the crowd. However, each contestant quickly rebounded and definitely would not make the same mistakes in their final run. This was going to be a very close competition.

While waiting for the final scores, I seemed to block everything out by thinking back to my early carefree kennel days and recalling how very easy things were at that time. I also remembered the difficulties encountered when first meeting my new family, entering the sorority house and causing a great degree of destruction.

My breathing was getting rapid due to my anxiety over the impact of this competition. While forcing myself to breathe normally and not fall prey to a panic attack, I recalled all of the good times I shared with my family once we got to know each other, the pride I experienced while in my public outings, the new friends who became a part of my life and all the service dogs who were here today to wish me well. Remembering my past and how those experiences shaped my life actually seemed to help...especially with my breathing since I was bordering on gasping. I was so momentarily overcome with anxiety over major career choices that I couldn't even remember my name. In the midst of this unwanted fog of nervousness, I experienced an unexpected moment of clarity as Kessen's advice to "follow my heart" echoed in my mind. Suddenly, I knew exactly what I wanted for my career...win or lose. Remembering my past was definitely the key to seeing my future.

While I was gradually recovering from my hazy trip down memory lane, hearing my mom calling my name brought me out of my mental fog. (*At least I remembered my name!*) The competition ended, the scores were tallied, and the

Someone was calling me.

judges were heading toward us with the championship trophy, the first, second and third place ribbons. Would they place that blue ribbon around my neck, and would it determine my future career? All of the time, effort, energy and work didn't matter anymore...I knew exactly what was right for me, and all of the frills associated with winning were irrelevant. As the judges came closer and closer, a feeling of calmness settled over me and replaced the earlier panic that filled my mind. Even the outcome really didn't matter anymore because either way, I was a winner...

PART III
THE DESTINATION
(The Present Day)

The championship competition that was meant to be the answer to all of my dreams occurred in what seemed like a blink of an eye. I missed a great deal of it due to the heightened anxiety that clouded my mind. Apparently, my auto-pilot (*I didn't even know I had one!*) kicked in and completed the course twice in record time without my being in full control of my senses. I'm sure the numerous practice runs and endless training sessions had something to do with it as well, but I don't remember most of the actual competition. That was quite a shame since I worked so hard to get to that place in time.

Due to the stress of the competition, my anxiety-ridden mind played tricks on me by replaying bits and pieces of my life while awaiting the judges' decisions. Reliving events in my life from the time I was a young pup living in the kennel with my siblings to the events leading up to today's competition put everything in perspective. Sometime during that experience, I made my career decision. In doing that, it no longer mattered if I won or lost the competition. My life changed significantly in those moments, and nothing would change my mind. I did exactly what Kessen advised me to do and followed my heart. That was all it took for my choice, and the rest would surely fall into place.

I changed so much over the fifteen months due to the people and dogs who influenced my life. For as long as I can remember, I dreamt of becoming a champion athlete. I wasn't sure what type of champion I would be; I just knew I had to train every day to accomplish my dream. I was pretty self-centered back then, but I was alone and accountable only to myself. All of my siblings had gone off in different directions…Calm went with a family to be their forever pet, and Calmer, later named Palmer, went to Arizona to train for possible assistance as a future career. Consequently, I was on my own in the kennel when this extraordinary family came into my life. While I'd like to say that I changed their lives, they really changed mine.

The entire household, lovingly referred to as the sorority house, embraced me as a member of their family. I came to their house having no one and wanting a different direction in my life. Because of their acceptance and tolerance over time, that house became my home…all because of them. They were and always would be my forever family.

I finally have a forever family!

We got off to a rocky start together due to my enthusiastic arrival to their house. (*They called it my chaotic arrival!*) Sure, I ricocheted off structures, turned over food bowls and ran the Indy 500 around their furniture in the living room. What can I say? I was an energetic pup! In wanting them to see my potential as an athlete, I somehow became a weapon of mass destruction. In hindsight, I was also probably terrified of having an actual family want me in spite of my aptitude for demolition. Perhaps I was afraid to get too attached to them for fear of them sending me back to the kennel. Whenever we passed by the post office, I crossed my paws in hopes that they wouldn't stop and drop me off. Fortunately for me, that never happened.

In spite of my racing through their house, bouncing off walls and closed doors (*Why didn't they just keep the doors open?*) and causing all sorts of problems, they still loved me. Even my *zooming* through the house at top speeds didn't deter them from continued acceptance into their family. At first I thought their tolerance of me demonstrated their ability to withstand pain, but I later learned that they just accepted me as I was… a rambunctious pup who bounced well!

My challenge with them was to make their dream for my future the same as mine. For that to happen, they had to recognize my potential as a winning athlete. The down side was that they were preparing me for a career as an assistance dog which was the opposite extreme from my own goal. I wasn't opposed to helping others, but it just didn't fit into my career plan. Somehow, I had to convince them that my dreams came first, and I had fifteen months to change their minds. Back then, it seemed like enough time to convince them of my dreams. I wasn't worried but should have been because the time really flew by.

Even though we shared a language barrier, the folks were good-natured and fair. Their dogs, on the other paw, presented very different challenges. I couldn't fool the dogs since we spoke the same language, and nothing got past Kessen, the leader of the pack. When we first met, I thought he was a pretentious pooch who over-estimated his role as the pack leader. He, in turn, thought I was an ill-behaved ruffian. Brightie, the blonde bombshell and next in line in the pack, was my mischievous soul mate. She enjoyed my antics as much as Kessen resented them. In time, we learned a lot about each other, accepted our differences and shared our hopes

They work well together.

and dreams. Even though it took a while, the three of us became great friends.

Kessen and Brightie were my mentors during my stay at the sorority house. Each had a different approach to life, but getting a variety of views gave me more options for my behavior. Kessen, the strong, regal pack leader had definite views of appropriate behavior while in the house and in public. Brightie wavered a bit on those rules and often found herself in many mischievous situations. Nevertheless, those differences allowed them to work together, and their beliefs rubbed off on me. I learned to appreciate proper behavior in public due to Kessen's no-nonsense approach to public etiquette. Through Brightie, I discovered how to laugh at myself when things went wrong and to take risks...even if it meant being sanctioned by a family member or worse... incurring Kessen's wrath. Each day was a learning experience for all of us.

What did they learn from me? Well, they didn't learn how to bounce off walls and doors...that's for sure. Kessen told me that he learned patience from me. No matter how much he pressured me as the pack leader, I never gave up my dreams. Because of my willingness to compromise and give both assistance and athletic dreams a chance, he allowed me to make my own decisions regarding career choices. That was such an important concession on Kessen's part. He wasn't one to budge easily in terms of his beliefs because his role as pack leader relied on his consistent adherence to rules and regulations. Being the pack leader was a tough job.

Brightie realized that having me as her soul mate was like having a twin sibling. She lived vicariously through my antics, but never suffered the consequences of my ill-advised

We'll always be soul mates.

behavior. Brightie could watch, laugh and walk away unscathed from the penalties of my reckless activities. In Brightie's world, that was a pretty good deal. On the other paw, Brightie also felt my sadness when some parts of my dreams came to an end and was always there to offer comfort during my unhappy moments. Soul mates did that for each other, and I knew in my heart that she would be a part of me forever.

As my time with my family was coming to an end, this past week was spent saying goodbye to all the people who embraced me during my stay here at the sorority house. Tomorrow, they were taking me to Advanced Training or Puppy College as it is called. I was happily entering the training program for a career as an assistance dog. Since all I talked about for the last fifteen months was a career as a champion athlete, my friends were totally shocked at my decision. Just as Kessen had a hunch that I would change my mind and choose assistance, he made sure that I looked at family and friends in the arena the day of the event to reinforce his intuition.

Seeing Deon, Kelyna and Carlita proudly wearing their capes presented clear-cut reminders of future possibilities as an assistance dog. Although Brightie wasn't too surprised, she wasn't quite as certain as Kessen was in terms of what my decision would be. Since she was thoroughly into canine feng shui, she was secretly hoping for a least a few blue ribbons hanging on my kennel walls before I went in the direction of assistance. For her, a little feng shui went a long way towards harmony in life.

Saying goodbye to all the people who were a part of my journey was a bit tough on all of us. The first thing in the morning, the folks took me to our usual church for the morning service. Following Mass, my favorite priest blessed me on my journey toward service to the disabled. He blessed each of the dogs raised by my folks, but I felt that his blessing for me was extra special. He even had a few tears in his eyes when we left. On the way out, I looked for the renowned Holy Water Fountain that Brightie wanted me to see. I had never seen it before because we never exited the services through this particular door. Apparently, after Kessen was blessed by the same priest before he went off to Puppy College, he attempted to drink from that Holy Water Fountain on his way out of the church.

That's where the stories differed. Kessen said that he was able to get a good gulp of water, but Brightie said that due to our mom's quick leash correction, Kessen didn't even come close to a sip. Both versions were funny, and I had to admit that water flowing in and out looked mighty inviting. I'll bet it was thoroughly refreshing as well! Nevertheless, I didn't take the chance on a repeat of Kessen's puppy behavior since he'd probably be very disappointed in my doing it. Brightie, enjoying the thrills of mischief-making, would love it!

We then visited our favorite restaurant, and having the managers and staff say their farewells brought tears to everyone's eyes. All of the staff members from the animal hospital came out to give me hugs and good wishes as well. Friends came to the house to do the same, and again, tears flowed. Cousin Carolyn brought Riggins for a final farewell.

He and I ran around the yard pretending that it wasn't the last time we'd see each other. However, I think we both secretly knew that it was the last time we'd run and play together as a couple.

Our planned future together was something for our imaginations to cling to while going our separate ways in life. Seeing him leave through that back gate with Cousin Carolyn just tugged at my heart. All in all, that last day at the sorority house was a day filled with a lot of hugs and all sorts

It just wasn't meant to be.

of emotions...mostly needing tissue for the tears. Brightie attempted to lighten the moment by running around the house and shredding tissue, but her only accomplishment was making a mess.

The sun was shining brightly the next morning as the household awakened and prepared for the journey to Puppy College. The entire family was going, and the folks were busy organizing dog bowls, dog food, treats, water, toys, collars and leashes for all of us. I was so glad that Kessen and Brightie were coming along on this trip. I wanted them with me for as long as I could. There was a motel not far from the training facility, and we'd stay there for the night. I've never stayed in a motel before, so that would really be exciting. Tomorrow they would all take me to Puppy College, and a new chapter in my life would begin.

Safety first...fun later.

We all piled into the Blue Baron, and our playful antics were curtailed by our secured car harnesses. My mom said something about the harnesses preventing our becoming canine projectiles if involved in an accident, but none of us knew what that meant. We just knew that our fun was over! Anyway, as the car started down the driveway, I looked back for the last time at the house that became my home...the only home I ever knew. I remembered how anxious I was when I first arrived, and now how very sad I was to leave the security I found within those walls.

As the car turned off the driveway, I was overwhelmed by what I saw. The dogs of the neighborhood stood in their driveways to say their goodbyes to me. Sammy, sitting upright in his driveway, gave me his nod of approval as we passed his house. I will miss his wisdom but will remember his advice in the years to come.

Stay safe!

On the other side of the street was Finnegan pacing back and forth in his driveway barking out his good bye to me. To him, I'll always be known as Toots! He also mentioned that he was sure that I was definitely going to miss him in my life. What a first-rate clown! But that clown was definitely right. I would certainly miss him and his antics. Yet, as silly as he was pretending to be, I knew he was sorry to see me leave the neighborhood. After all, I'm the only dog who laughed at his jokes!

See ya, Toots!

Other dogs were lined up along the way, and each gave a special goodbye nod, bark or howl. When we reached the end of the block, there was Kaiser, our neighborhood sentinel. As the car drove by, Kaiser stood up and gave a majestic bow in my direction. Since I was strapped in by this car harness, I wasn't able to return the bow. However, I did nod my thanks to him for his kind gesture and for the work he did for the

Good Luck!

neighborhood. As we passed him and the car turned off my street, I knew that I was leaving my life here behind me. I, too, needed tissue at this moment.

Once we hit the highway, exhaustion overcame me, and I immediately fell asleep. Kessen and Brightie had been sound asleep for quite a long time. Once I awakened, I wanted to take in all of the sights and sounds of the trip. Since I was facing forward in the back seat and not in a crate facing backwards, I could see where we were going before we even got there. That was a whole lot better than my first trip when I faced the back of the car. The scenery is a whole lot better facing forward! Thankfully, we never had to visit that most unusual rest stop.

Even though we were restrained in our harnesses, arriving at the motel, which wasn't far from the training facility, was exciting. After our dad checked us in for the night, we were unhitched from the harnesses and went to the room together. We felt a bit sorry for our dad since he had to bring all of our stuff into the room, but he used something called a cart that carried everything at one time. He sure was a smart man to have found something like that! The folks brought their sandwiches in a cooler with additional vegetables to include in our dinner. They were so good to us.

The folks needed ice to cool their drinks, so I accompanied my mom to a room down the hall that had something called an ice machine. (*Humans really have it easy!*) She had me wear my cape since it was one of the last times I would wear it with her, and I was proud to oblige. On the way down the hall, I spotted another individual with a dog who was wearing the same type of cape as mine. They were also heading toward the room with the ice machine. That dog must be going into Puppy College tomorrow as well. There was something so familiar about that dog, but I couldn't quite put my paw on it. He was much taller than I, but seeing his coal-black coat and distinctive shape of his head tugged at my memory. Since we were all heading to the same place, I'd get

I've missed him so much.

a closer look when we got there and might remember where I'd seen him before.

As usual, curiosity was overcoming me. As we got to the room with the ice machine, I stopped and took a good look at him. He, in turn, looked intently at me. In the instant that our eyes met, we recognized each other. It was Calmer…my brother! Of course, he was now named Palmer, but here was my brother who went to Arizona to train for a career in assistance. What was he doing here in this motel?

As my mom and his handler exchanged information about the possible connection between us, Palmer and I nuzzled each other lovingly for quite a while. As it turned out, Palmer and his handler traveled from Arizona and were staying at this motel for the night since Palmer was starting Puppy College tomorrow. They were so happy that we were not only reunited but going to Puppy College together. What a wonderful twist of fate! I knew that someday I would see him again, and now the circle was complete. We had to say good night for now, but my mom and Palmer's handler agreed to meet at breakfast so we could share some time together again. Who knew that going to the ice machine would change my life?

When we got back to the room, I told Kessen and Brightie all about seeing Palmer again. They were so happy for me and couldn't wait to meet him tomorrow. After going outside for the night, we were ready to go to sleep. I was about to go into my portable canvas kennel when the surprise of all surprises happened. The folks invited me to sleep on the bed with them. Dogs in training were never allowed on the furniture, but since it was my last night with them, they gave me that gift. It was pretty crowded in that bed with all five of us, but it was another great memory to store close to my heart.

The next day, the folks met Palmer's handler for breakfast while Palmer and I shared our experiences. Since he and I were going to Puppy College at the same time, we might also be kennel mates. That would be so wonderful and would help with the loss of leaving my forever family. I didn't want to think of that moment, but it was coming sooner than I realized.

As we drove to the training facility, all of my previous bravado left me. The realization that I was leaving my family hit me. They were trying not to show their sadness because it would travel down the leash and make things worse for me. But, I saw the unhappiness in their faces as well as a few tears that dropped down from their eyes.

While in the car, both Kessen and Brightie nuzzled me and wished me well in this next chapter of my journey. Kessen told me that he was so proud of me and of the dog I had become. Those words meant so very much to me, and I would treasure them for as long as I lived. He wasn't that pompous dog from that first day of my arrival...he was my mentor, and above all, he was my friend. Brightie told me that we'd always be connected in life because we were soul mates, and soul mates never lost contact with each other.

Oh, by the way...I won the competition by a very slight margin, and the folks placed my first place trophy on the mantle above their fireplace. Kessen and Brightie hardly ever went into that room which is why they didn't see where the folks placed it before we left. I hoped that seeing it in that position of honor would surprise them when they returned from the trip. That trophy was a reminder of the black tornado whose life was changed due to the unconditional love given to an ill-behaved ruffian. That was Kessen's earlier description of me and not mine. In hindsight, his assessment of me wasn't entirely incorrect.

Brightie was in for a special surprise as well. Little did she know that when she returned home, she would find my first place blue ribbon hanging on her kennel wall. After all, I wanted her to have a special remembrance of me, and she deserved a little canine feng shui for harmony in her life.

She's going to love her surprise.

I knew the folks were as sad to see me go as I was to leave them. Last night before we went to sleep, Kessen told me about a special ritual that the folks shared amongst themselves when giving up a dog to Puppy College. It was such a sad occasion for them because each dog became a beloved family member and giving them up was so very difficult. But, their ritual was meant for the dog's well-being and not theirs. Since they trained each dog to maintain eye contact with whoever held the leash, the expectation was for the dog to happily transfer his eye contact to the trainer without any signs of apprehension. If the dog continued walking with the trainer and didn't look back at the folks in dismay, the folks had done their job in preparing the dog for the rigors of Puppy College. That ritual offered them a bit of solace in the midst of giving up the dog. So far, none of the dogs they trained ever looked back.

Kessen and Brightie stayed in the car after our final goodbyes. The folks hugged me, kissed me and slowly walked me toward the doors of the training facility. On the way, we met up with Palmer and his handler. Brother and sister were going to enter the world of assistance together, and wasn't that such a special event?

As we approached the facility, the new trainer came to the door and looked like a very kind man. In spite of that, I really wanted to look back when they handed my leash over to him just to say one more goodbye. But, I remembered what Kessen had told me about their ritual and knew that if I did, they would feel that they didn't do their best for me in my training. Even with tears in my eyes, I pretended to go willingly and happily with the new trainer. As much as I wanted to look back at them for the last time, I fought the urge to do it. Instead, I gave my folks the only gift I had to offer...my signature helicopter wag of the tail reserved for very special people. In seeing that unique wag of the tail, they'd know exactly what I meant and how I felt about them.

Palmer and I entered the facility together…tails wagging and looking forward to the next chapters in our lives.

I've heard it said that the journey, itself, was what made the destination worthwhile. What began as my quest for athletic glory became a mere stepping-stone through the twists and turns of life. Due to the unconditional love of my family and good friends, my journey took me in an entirely new direction. As a final result, my destination changed significantly. That newly discovered destination became not only the beginning of an entrance to the world of assistance to others but also to the beginning of a life worth living…

This is what I was born to do.

CONCLUSION

As I watched Izzy telling her story, I felt such pride in the kind of dog she had become. She now demonstrated such grace and poise while sharing her experiences with my deck listeners. Even with its most unusual beginning, Izzy's telling of her story kept them on the edge of their paws with hackles dancing all over the place. Everyone was so eager to hear more about her adventures. As she spoke, they responded with such enthusiasm...often in the form of barks and howls. Their appreciation echoed loudly into the night. From a distance, dogs in the neighborhood joined in the howling not even knowing what they were howling about...it was just a fun thing to do at night. I'm sure those who were asleep didn't appreciate the interruption, but the dogs enjoyed it.

She's an inspiration to us all.

As Izzy's story ended with her entrance to Puppy College, she explained how her training there would prepare her for a career in assistance...a career very different from her initial plan for athletic glory. She was happy with her decision, had followed her heart and never looked back.

Signaling the end of her tale, Izzy bowed politely and thanked both the audience and me for allowing her to share her journey with us this evening.

Looking directly into the eyes of her enthusiastic audience, Izzy encouraged each one of them to become dreamers. In her opinion, dreamers lived exciting, fun-filled lives. Her life was full of adventures because of her dreams. Even though her vision changed along the way, the outcome was still a wish fulfilled. According to Izzy, believing in yourself was the key to making dreams come true.

That being said, she offered another gracious bow to her listeners and went back toward the patio doors leading to the house. The moonlight streaking through the tree branches spotlighted her exit and intensified her shadow as it followed behind her. While that gave it a bit of a creepy, yet dramatic exit, the listeners once again barked and howled their approval. This story was evidently a tremendous hit for them. Even I, as the resident storyteller in the neighborhood, never got two barking and howling ovations!

Since our guest storyteller was only staying with us for the weekend, we were very fortunate that she was able to share her story with us this evening. On Monday, Izzy would resume her position as a service dog for her partner in a wheel chair. While she definitely had a flare for storytelling, assistance to others was her true calling.

The listeners continued to mingle on the deck engaging each other in conversations about her story. It was like a deck version of a book club. Maybe I should start one following each story...call it Story Club and have discussions following the event. That might be fun, and getting various opinions of a story might be fascinating. Then again, I wasn't the best at accepting criticism, but I'm sure that would never occur. I'll have to consider the introduction of Story Club to the group on our next storytelling night.

The conversations continued with talk of the sadness experienced by Izzy leaving her siblings, her chaotic arrival at the sorority house, the struggle to overcome communication issues with her new mom and dad as well as blending in to a new canine pack with a staunch leader and a mischievous cohort. What was interesting was that some of the dogs experienced similar situations in their lives and thoroughly related to Izzy's dilemmas. Hearing their comments assured me that Izzy made her story come to life for her listeners, and some even shared some of her issues. She reached her audience with her heart-felt words, and what a wonderful accomplishment that was for her.

As the dogs slowly left the deck area for their own homes, I sat on the deck for a while lost in my thoughts about this evening's events. Izzy's stay with us as a pup really changed our lives in so many ways. She mentioned that she learned a lot from us, and we, in turn, learned from her. However, all of us missed a very important point…each of us used first impressions as an indicator of character. In doing that, we unintentionally made judgments about each other.

When she first arrived, I thought of her as a dark funnel cloud descending upon our peaceful sorority house. Her frenzied behavior ended the tranquility of our home, and I labeled her an ill-disciplined ruffian before I even got to

I was labeled a ruffian.

know her. Brightie gave her the benefit of the doubt since she recognized Izzy's behavior as very similar to hers in terms of mischief making. In that respect, Brightie's assessment was much nicer than mine. The folks, on the other paw, didn't know what to think other than their next fifteen months were going to be spent with this enthusiastic yet apparent weapon of mass destruction.

Izzy made her judgments as well. In her opinion, I was a pompous pack leader who thought only of strict adherence to rules and regulations. Things with me were either right or wrong...no discussion. She thought of Brightie as a follower who functioned under the hard-lined paw of the pack leader, and you know who that was! Izzy even made judgments about our mom and dad by initially naming them Bad Cop and Good Cop. Sure, she changed the names later, but Izzy's original names for them were based upon first impressions... just as our snap judgments were made of her.

We were all very wrong to do that even though I don't believe it was intentional. By getting to know each other, we learned that it wasn't the right thing to do. First impressions were actually snap judgments and definitely not true indicators of one's character. Finding that out took time, patience and understanding. Izzy's stay with us gave us more than we bargained for in many ways. The most important learning experience was a life lesson in terms of first impressions...that being, it's important to get to know someone before forming an opinion.

I was exhausted by all that transpired this evening and was anxious to get to my kennel for some well-deserved sleep. As I walked through the sunroom on my way to the kitchen, I noticed that the furniture in various rooms was somewhat rearranged. My hackles automatically went on full alert. Sometime during the storytelling evening, the folks positioned gates in various parts of the house. In the corner of the kitchen was a small, wire kennel with lowered food bowls next to it. A plastic box full of small squeak toys and some rubber bones was on the other side of the kitchen kennel, and another small kennel was placed in the dining area. These were all signs of impending trouble.

I found Brightie hiding in her own kennel and staring at the awesome blue ribbon left there by Izzy as a token of their friendship. She knew why I was coming to see her and was hoping that the canine feng shui created by the ribbon would somehow protect her from the inevitable.

It was apparent that another pup was coming to the sorority house. We've been fooled in the past because of our lack of situational awareness but not this time. Those gates, crates, food bowls and toys were screaming NEW PUPPY COMING! Perhaps, the newcomer was just staying for a weekend visit. Maybe, we're just overacting to the situation. Best to get a good night's rest and get the facts in the morning.

After a restless night, morning came and Brightie and I raced to the kitchen to get an assessment of future events. The folks told us that we were in for a treat because the Aunties were coming for a visit. The Aunties were not only good friends of our folks but also our puppy sitters when the folks went to pick up another puppy. Auntie Deb and Auntie Brenda really loved staying with us and

We had great fun with the Aunties.

often played a lot of games with us. Auntie Deb taught me the "sniffing game" years ago. She'd get on her hands and knees and spin around on the carpet while I'd try to sniff out what sort of treat she had in her hand. It was glorious fun. However, I can't do that anymore because the excitement of the game causes me to have an attack of reverse sneezing. Once that issue started, it was difficult for me to stop sneezing, so we don't play that game anymore. But, we still have lots of fun.

Nevertheless, having them visit meant another puppy was coming to the sorority house. The Socialization Squad would once again be mobilized into service. Brightie and I would begin another tour of duty with this newcomer...rules, regulations and appropriate behavior would overshadow the premises. Attempting to lighten the moment, Brightie jokingly promised to protect me if the situation got threatening. Truth be told...even as the pack leader, I'd allow her to do that. After all, the leader must be protected.

Countering Brightie's attempt at humor, I mentioned to her that this situation might not be too bad. Izzy had been quite a challenge, and things worked out with her...after a while. This attitude of mine really frightened Brightie because I was rarely optimistic about anything. Known for my pessimistic approach to life, this change in attitude was apparently shielding the apprehension I felt. I reassured Brightie that we'd face this new puppy together, and challenges only made us stronger. Brightie was really frightened now!

In the meantime, the Aunties played with us, let us run around the yard and took us for a walk in the neighborhood. When they brought us home, Brightie and I settled into restful naps near the back door. We didn't want to be caught off guard when the folks arrived with the puppy. Hearing a car pull up in the driveway awakened us. While we heard the garage door slowly moving upward along its rails, we each braced ourselves in a sitting position for the moment that back door opened.

Those first moments were critical in terms of our assessment of the months to come, but we weren't going to allow first impressions to totally cloud our minds. We learned that from the Izzy experience. An open mind allowed for more than the first impression to determine one's character, and we would be mindful of that in dealing with this newcomer.

Why was it taking so long for them to come in? Was the puppy already struggling with the folks? Should we run for cover? Our imaginations were going wild just as our upright hackles traveled up and down our bodies. Since our hackles weren't concentrating on just the neck area and instead going back and forth from neck to tail, they sensed something more than just excitement. Something was about to happen.

As the door knob slowly turned, the door creaked as it gradually opened. In doing that, it lent a very creepy element to the situation. What happened next made us gasp for air and start moving slowly backwards from our sitting position. Our eyes dilated to saucer-like proportions as our hearts skipped numerous beats sounding like thunder in our ears. Even Brightie attempted to use me as a shield from what was to come. So much for her protecting me!

Staring at us from the darkness of the garage were eyes that actually appeared to glow in the dark. Suddenly, razor sharp teeth illuminated the pup's mouth due to their whiteness against an ebony coat. The entire image was terribly frightening to imaginations already gone wild. The pup stepped tentatively into the house and stared up at us with those smoldering eyes. Brightie, peeking out from behind me, took one last look and quickly retreated to the other side of the house where it was safe. I, alone, was left to face off with the newcomer and would do that for the next fifteen months.

Was this puppy's frightening entry just a figment of my imagination or a foreshadowing of ominous experiences in the months to come? Only time would tell. Nevertheless, this particular newcomer's entrance to the sorority house promises numerous exciting stories to share in the future. For you, my valued readers, it is another story waiting to be told...

Until we meet again...

The Host

My name is Kessen, and I live with my mom, dad and best friend Brightie in a suburb of Chicago, Illinois. While I value my role as the resident storyteller in the neighborhood, I served as the host for this particular story since it was appropriate for Izzy to tell her story as only she could tell it.

In my free time, I like fooling around with Brightie, running around the yard with my ring toy, taking long walks in the neighborhood with my dad, going on car rides and working with the pups who cross the threshold of our home that we lovingly call the sorority house. Serving as Co-Captain of the Socialization Squad with Brightie, I also enjoy mentoring new puppies as they learn the appropriate behaviors necessary for the world of assistance. I look forward to the next pup who joins our family in preparation for a life of service to others. That adventure promises fun, excitement and lots of special treats.

The Guest Storyteller

My name is Izzy, and I'm now living the pampered life of a princess in a suburb of Chicago, Illinois. A family is so important, but mine is extra special. I was fortunate enough to be adopted by the one person who gave me that special *tingle* reminiscent of my birth mother's love. Yes, Auntie Fran adopted me and became my new mom. Now, I get that special *tingle* every minute of my life with her. I also have a special connection with Michael, her husband, who loves me dearly. In return for that cherished bond, I call him Daddy.

My life is full of adventures while exploring my wonderful yard and taking in all of the scents and aromas of the changing seasons. Since Riggins and I were reunited, we spend quite a lot of time together running around in the yard and seeking out intruding birds and squirrels. When exhausted from that, we take time to munch on leaves, juicy grass and any flowers that might prove attractive at the moment. We spend so much time together that "The Rigg-zzys" is our new, well-deserved name!

It was our destiny.

When not playing with Riggins, I enjoy long walks with the folks, retrieving thrown balls, getting special treats, and best of all, sleeping next to Mom. My family means the world to me, and while it took me a while to figure things out, the absolute truth is that dreams really do come true.

The Author

Jennifer Rae Trojan, who writes as Jennifer Rae, lives in a suburb of Chicago, Illinois with her husband Chuck and two dogs named Kessen and Brightie. Since retirement as high school guidance counselors, Jennifer and Chuck have worked with various assistance organizations serving as puppy sitters, puppy raisers and volunteers with animal assisted therapy. In addition to those activities, Jennifer gives presentations at libraries, in schools and to community groups regarding the journey of the assistance dog and how it relates to the writing of her books. Chuck, Kessen and Brightie accompany her to these presentations representing three of the characters from her books.

Jennifer and her husband consider being a part of a potential assistance dog's journey a privilege, an adventure and a true labor of love. The entire family looks forward to their next puppy.

Acknowledgements

Fostering a puppy for possible assistance, training a therapy dog, rescuing a shelter dog or raising a well-behaved pet are not easy tasks. They are joint efforts among owners, families, friends, relatives, trainers and even strangers who lend assistance throughout these endeavors.

While I thank all of those people who have assisted with training and socialization, there are certain individuals who need special recognition for their efforts with Izzy. As a bit of a twist, I've attempted to make my "thanks" a bit more personal by adding their faces to their names.

First and foremost, I must thank my extraordinary husband **Chuck Trojan** for his support, enthusiasm and assistance while writing this story. Without his enduring love, endless encouragement and countless proof reading, this story would not have been written nor published.

Mary Krystinak, whose computer wizardry in terms of formatting and organizing, brought my story to life in the form of this book. I am ever so grateful for her remarkable computer expertise and endless patience while working with me. In addition to those qualities, I am especially fortunate to call her my friend.

Stephanie D. Ascencio, of Schmoopsie Pet Photography, graciously granted permission for use of the cover photos on Izzy's book. Those incredible photos demonstrate Stephanie's skill in capturing Izzy's expressions. Her talent and generosity are greatly appreciated She also contributed to the initial mockup and designs of the covers.

Many thanks to **Pam Osbourne** who not only served as a consultant to the book but was instrumental in the final printing process including the formatting of the cover photos. Her expertise and talents were so numerous and greatly appreciated. She's awesome!

Carol (Auntie Carol) **DeMaio**, a valued friend of many years, served as one of my proof readers. She not only critiqued the numerous pages, but also tolerated reading the various versions of Izzy's story prior to my final manuscript. Her productive insights as well as constructive criticisms provided invaluable assistance toward the completion of this story. I truly appreciate her time, efforts, expertise and above all, her enduring friendship.

Kathleen Deist, who I lovingly refer to as The Goddess of Grammar and Punctuation, also served as a proof reader for this story. Her suggestions proved extremely helpful in the preparation for the book's publication. Having her as a consultant was awesome; but having her as my friend is the greater gift.

Kelly Jatczak of P.S. Advertising, Inc. was responsible for the design and creation of business cards, banners, car magnets and mailing labels for this book as well as for my first book, *Kessen's Kronikles, The Adventures of a Cross Country Canine*. Her creativity far

surpassed my expectations, and I'm truly grateful for her contributions.

Fran (Auntie Fran) and **Michael Saltarelli** gave Izzy the extraordinary gift of a forever family. My husband and I are so very grateful for their

unconditional love for her. Giving Izzy the life of a pampered princess is icing on the cake…not just for Izzy, but for us as well.

I thank **Carolyn** (Cousin Carolyn) **Doebler** and her wonderful husband **Adam** for being such an important part of Izzy's life. They not only introduced Izzy to their Golden Retriever Riggins but also gave her the gift of another caring family. Izzy's life is filled with love from so many special people and a best friend named Riggins.

Steven (Cousin Steven) **Saltarelli** has a very unique relationship with all animals. This connection draws animals to him in a most extraordinary and remarkable way. While Izzy thoroughly adores him, Steven still won't let her play with his rabbits.

Deb Steller and Brenda Whitesell (The Aunties) are the best of friends and assist with the socialization of each of the dogs in training. Their help as puppy sitters in our absences give each dog an opportunity to experience their companionship, training and love. Entrusting the dogs to anyone but their Aunties is not an option.

Jan Jaeger of Charlotte, North Carolina, became my good friend years ago when we both raised siblings for an assistance dog organization. As a certified dog trainer, Jan's insight into animal behavior and exceptional training methods make her a most valuable resource when working with dogs. In addition to those qualities, she is my major source of laughter from across the miles. We continue to laugh, train and compare notes with each dog we raise. Bless her heart.

The trainers at **Narnia Pet Behavior and Training Center** have provided exceptional guidance not just for Izzy,

but for all of the dogs we raised. **Joy Rittierodt** with the assistance of **Rachel Woodward** and **Nivin Wynn** shared their expertise through instruction, lively demonstrations and individual attention during each of their classes. Their knowledge of dog behavior and training is immeasurable. In addition, the classes were a lot of fun...not just for the dogs, but for the handlers as well.

For many years, **Panera Bread** has been a major advocate for assistance dogs in training. Managers like **Vince Palmisano** and **Don Hansen** have welcomed the dogs into their establishment. In doing that, they assisted in the dogs' journeys toward being silent guardians to the disabled. Turin, Kessen, Brightie, Marnie, Izzy and Tansy can't thank you enough!

 **Father Frank Vitus** and **Father Slawek Ignasik** are two of the priests who blessed the dogs before we took them to the Advanced Training program. Knowing that the dogs were beginning the next chapter in their lives with a

special blessing made giving them up just a bit easier.

Arizona's **Marge McCleod** and Palmer, her dog in training, met me at the ice machine the evening before our dogs were to enter Advanced Training. After a brief exchange of information due to our dogs' similarities, we learned that we had raised siblings. How very fitting that Izzy and Palmer would enter training together. Somehow family always finds a way to reconnect.

Special thanks to the **assistance organizations** across the country that provide puppies for fostering and to the **puppy raisers** who share in the puppy's journey. Fostering a puppy for potential service is one that lingers in the heart and mind forever.

Finally, I sincerely thank all **assistance dogs** for the work they do for others. On any given day, most of us can't even imagine how much they do to help others in need. Special treats for all of you!

In Memoriam

KESSEN
2005 – 2015

Just prior to the publication of this book, Kessen passed on ever so peacefully to the Rainbow Bridge. His memory will live on in our minds while his paw prints remain on our hearts forever. He was dearly loved by everyone.